# KASHYAPA: CHRONICLES OF SIGIRIYA

*The Novel*

## D. DECKKER

**Dinsu Books**

*To my beloved wife, Subhashini,*
*Your unwavering support, love, and belief in me make every*
*word I write possible. You are my partner in every journey, and*
*this book is as much yours as it is mine.*

*And to my precious daughter, Sasha,*
*You are the light of my life and my greatest inspiration. Your*
*boundless curiosity and joy remind me why stories matter.*

*This book is for both of you, with all my love.*

# CONTENTS

# INTRODUCTION

The Lion Rock of Sigiriya stands as one of history's greatest enigmas. Rising nearly 200 meters above the surrounding plains, this colossal fortress is a marvel of engineering and artistry, crowned with the ruins of a palace that once belonged to a king whose life is shrouded in legend.

Kashyapa, the king who built Sigiriya, is a figure both celebrated and condemned in the annals of Sri Lankan history. To some, he was a visionary ruler who created an awe-inspiring citadel of art and innovation. To others, he was a usurper, haunted by the shadow of his father's murder and consumed by a need to secure his legacy at all costs.

This story begins in the heart of ancient Sri Lanka, in a time when kingdoms were forged by ambition and undone by betrayal. The lush forests and emerald hills that now surround Sigiriya once bore witness to Kashyapa's rise and fall—a tale of power, paranoia, and passion.

In these pages, we journey into the world of Kashyapa: a man of great contradictions, torn between his desires and his demons. From the construction of the magnificent fortress to the political intrigue of his court, we delve into a narrative where ambition collides with destiny, and the weight of guilt shapes the course of an empire.

While history provides the foundation for this tale, much of what follows is a work of fiction. The ruins of Sigiriya speak volumes about the ingenuity of its creators but remain silent on the man behind its glory. This novel seeks to fill those silences, imagining the inner world of a king who dared to defy the gods and the ghosts of his past.

Welcome to the chronicles of Kashyapa. His story awaits.

# PREFACE

The story of Kashyapa and Sigiriya is one that has fascinated historians, archaeologists, and storytellers for centuries. Towering above the lush jungles of Sri Lanka, Sigiriya is more than just an architectural marvel; it is a monument shrouded in mystery, ambition, and tragedy. What drove a king to build such a breathtaking fortress atop a rock? What secrets lie hidden within its walls, its frescoes, and its silent ruins?

In this novel, I have sought to breathe life into the legend of Kashyapa, blending historical accounts with imaginative storytelling. While Sigiriya itself stands as a testament to human ingenuity, its history offers a canvas upon which themes of power, betrayal, and redemption can be explored.

Though this tale is rooted in the rich heritage of Sri Lanka, it is a work of fiction. I have taken creative liberties to craft a story that delves into the humanity of Kashyapa, the burden of his choices, and the timeless struggle between ambition and conscience.

As you turn these pages, I invite you to step into the shadowed halls of Sigiriya, to walk beside a king haunted by his past and driven by his dreams, and to uncover the secrets of a time where power and fate intertwined.

This book is not just a story about a king—it is a reflection on legacy, the price of greatness, and the indomitable spirit of those who seek to leave their mark on the world.

I hope you find as much wonder in this tale as I did in writing it.

With gratitude,
D. Deckker

# CHAPTER 1: THE COUP

The air inside Anuradhapura's royal chamber was thick with incense and treachery. Shadows flickered on the polished stone walls, cast by the golden lamps that encircled the grand hall. The room, once a sanctum of solemn rituals and declarations, now hummed with an unspoken tension, broken only by the faint rustle of robes as courtiers and guards exchanged uneasy glances. At the heart of it all stood Kashyapa, tall and unyielding, his features carved with the sharp edges of ambition and defiance.

"Father," Kashyapa began, his voice calm yet edged with steel. He took a step closer to the stone dais where King Dhatusena sat, regal yet diminished. The once-mighty monarch's face, weathered by years of rule and betrayal, was set in an expression of quiet disdain.

"Do not call me that," Dhatusena spat, his voice low but brimming with fury. "You forfeited that right the moment you conspired with those jackals." His gaze flicked to the cluster of nobles lurking at the edges of the room, their expressions inscrutable.

Kashyapa's jaw tightened, but he did not waver. "This is not about them," he said. "This is about the kingdom. Our kingdom."

He gestured toward the gilded walls and the intricate tapestries that adorned them, depicting battles won and alliances forged. "What you have hoarded for yourself could strengthen our armies, fortify our borders, ensure our legacy."

Dhatusena's laughter was bitter and hollow, echoing in the vast chamber. "Legacy? You think building walls and buying swords will preserve our name? Foolish boy. Legacy is carved in the hearts of men, not in stone or gold."

"Enough!" Kashyapa's voice thundered, silencing the murmurs that had begun to ripple through the hall. "The treasure, Father. Tell me where it is."

Dhatusena rose slowly, his movements deliberate, his presence still commanding despite the betrayal that surrounded him. "You wish to know where my treasure lies?" he said, his voice laced with scorn. "It lies in the Kalawewa—the great irrigation tank I built for our people. That is my legacy."

For a moment, the hall was silent, the air taut as a bowstring. Kashyapa's hands clenched into fists at his sides, his nails biting into his palms. He turned to the guards flanking the dais. "Take him," he ordered.

The soldiers hesitated, their loyalty caught between the man who had ruled them for decades and the prince who now held their futures in his grip. But the moment passed, and they moved to seize the king.

Dhatusena did not struggle. Instead, he fixed his son with a look that was both pitying and scornful. "You may take my throne," he said, his voice steady despite the chains that now bound his hands. "But you will never have my kingdom."

---

The news of Dhatusena's imprisonment spread like wildfire, igniting whispers in the streets and echoing through the corridors of the palace. Some spoke of Kashyapa's boldness, others of his betrayal. Among those who watched from the shadows was Moggallana, Dhatusena's younger son and the rightful heir to the throne.

In the dimly lit corridors of the palace, Moggallana confronted Kashyapa. His younger brother's eyes, wide with shock and fury, mirrored the fire that now consumed their family. "You've gone too far," Moggallana hissed, his voice trembling with rage. "Father trusted you, and you've turned on him like a rabid dog."

Kashyapa met his brother's gaze, unflinching. "And what would you have done, Moggallana? Waited as Father squandered our legacy on his pride? You know as well as I do that the throne demands strength."

"Strength?" Moggallana's voice rose, his fists clenching at his sides. "Strength is earned, Kashyapa. Not stolen."

"Leave," Kashyapa said, his tone cold and final. "If you stay, you will only share his fate."

Moggallana's lips curled into a snarl. "You think this is over? The people will see you for the traitor you are. And when they do, you'll wish you had never been born."

---

Days later, Kashyapa's throne room echoed with the sound of footsteps as the court assembled for the most contentious decision yet: Dhatusena's fate. The nobles, once silent conspirators, now voiced their opinions with veiled threats and cautious alliances.

"The king's presence in the dungeons is a danger to the throne," one noble said, his words carefully measured. "As long as he lives, he remains a symbol of resistance."

Another countered, "But to execute him would only incite rebellion. The people revere Dhatusena as a just ruler."

Kashyapa sat on the golden throne, his expression inscrutable. The weight of the crown on his brow felt heavier with each passing day.

Finally, he spoke. "The decision has already been made. Dhatusena will not leave the dungeons." His voice was firm, but the words seemed to hang in the air, echoing with unspoken doubt.

---

The day of Dhatusena's death was marked by an oppressive silence. The sun blazed mercilessly over Anuradhapura, as if bearing witness to the act that would forever alter the kingdom's course.

Kashyapa stood at the edge of the chamber where his father would meet his end. Dhatusena was dragged to a wall deep within the palace, his face calm, his dignity unbroken.

"You think this will secure your throne?" Dhatusena said, his voice unwavering even as mortar was brought forward. "The stones will remember this. So will the people."

Brick by brick, the wall rose, entombing the former king alive. His final words, muffled but resonant, echoed through the chamber as the last stone was set: "Kashyapa, your legacy will be one of ashes."

As the sun dipped below the horizon, casting the palace in shadow, Kashyapa returned to the throne room. His victory was complete, but it tasted of ash.

In the weeks that followed, whispers of a curse began to circulate. Some claimed to have seen Dhatusena's ghost wandering the halls, his eyes blazing with unfulfilled vengeance. Others spoke of unnatural occurrences—a sudden chill in the air, the flicker of lamps that had burned steadily for hours.

For Kashyapa, the throne he had seized with such determination now seemed to weigh heavier than ever. And as he sat in the gilded chair, staring into the shadows that danced across the walls, he could not shake the feeling that his father was watching, waiting.

---

The sounds of galloping hooves shattered the uneasy quiet of the night. A messenger burst into the palace, his face pale with urgency. "Prince Moggallana has fled the kingdom," he announced, falling to one knee before Kashyapa. "He seeks refuge in India."

Kashyapa's lips pressed into a thin line. He dismissed the messenger with a wave of his hand and rose from his throne. Crossing to the balcony, he gazed out over the city. The lights of Anuradhapura twinkled like distant stars, but they offered no solace.

"So it begins," he murmured, the weight of inevitability settling over him. He would fortify his rule, consolidate his power, and prepare for the day when Moggallana would return. For Kashyapa knew that the blood spilled in pursuit of the throne was only the beginning. The true battle was yet to come.

# CHAPTER 2: A NEW VISION

The throne room of Anuradhapura was a tableau of grandeur and unease. The golden throne, now occupied by Kashyapa, gleamed in the faint morning light that filtered through latticed windows. Incense curled lazily upward, unable to mask the tension that gripped the assembled court. The nobles, clad in their finest silk robes, exchanged wary glances, while the Buddhist monks, their saffron robes stark against the dark stone walls, sat silently, their expressions a mixture of disapproval and apprehension.

Kashyapa sat tall and still, his gaze sweeping across the room like a hawk surveying its prey. His victory over Dhatusena had secured his place on the throne, but the crown weighed heavier than he had imagined. The whispers of betrayal and the haunting echoes of his father's final words followed him like a shadow.

"Let it be known," Kashyapa's voice rang out, cutting through the murmurs like a blade, "that the capital of this kingdom will no longer reside in Anuradhapura. The city is too exposed, too vulnerable to the ambitions of those who wish to see us fall. Our future lies elsewhere."

The declaration hung in the air, a challenge thrown to the

assembled court. A ripple of shock moved through the room, quickly stifled by the weight of Kashyapa's presence. He allowed the silence to linger, his gaze fixed on the monks seated at the edge of the gathering.

One of them, a venerable elder named Thera Sanghamitta, rose slowly. His voice was calm but firm, carrying the weight of decades of spiritual authority. "Your Majesty, the sacred city of Anuradhapura has been the heart of our kingdom for centuries. To abandon it is to sever the lifeline of our faith and heritage. What place could rival its sanctity?"

Kashyapa's lips curled into a thin smile. **"Sigiriya,"** he said, the name rolling off his tongue with deliberate precision. "The Lion Rock. A fortress that will rise from the earth like a divine throne. It will not merely rival Anuradhapura; it will surpass it. A place of power, invincibility, and eternal legacy."

The murmurs returned, louder this time, as the nobles whispered among themselves. The monks exchanged troubled glances, their silence now laden with unspoken dissent.

"Your Majesty," Sanghamitta began, "Sigiriya is sacred land, once a haven for monks in meditation. To disturb it with the hammer and chisel of mortal ambition would invite the wrath of the divine."

Before Kashyapa could respond, a figure stepped forward from the shadows of the hall. Rajith, the royal architect, was a man of striking features—sharp cheekbones, piercing eyes, and a demeanor that exuded both brilliance and eccentricity. His robe, streaked with the dust of his trade, contrasted sharply with the opulence of the court.

"Your Majesty," Rajith said, his voice cutting through the growing unrest, "all great works begin with great ambition. Sigiriya is no mere rock; it is a canvas waiting to be transformed. Imagine it: a fortress that touches the sky, its walls adorned with the stories of your reign, its gardens flowing with water like veins of the earth itself. A monument to your glory and a warning to your enemies."

Kashyapa's eyes lit with intrigue, though he kept his expression measured. "Go on," he said.

Rajith stepped closer, unfurling a scroll he had carried. He laid it on the floor, revealing intricate sketches of a fortress unlike anything the court had ever seen. The drawings depicted a massive structure perched atop the rock, with spiraling staircases, cascading fountains, and frescoes that seemed to dance with life. The nobles leaned forward, their skepticism mingling with curiosity.

"The Lion Rock," Rajith continued, his voice rising with passion, "is the perfect foundation for a fortress that will stand for eternity. Its height will make it impregnable, its beauty will inspire awe, and its presence will remind all who see it that Kashyapa is a king chosen by the gods themselves."

Sanghamitta's voice cut through the moment. "Chosen by the gods, or defying them?" he asked, his tone heavy with warning. "Sigiriya is a place of meditation and sanctity. To reshape it for earthly power is to risk inviting a curse upon this kingdom."

Rajith turned to the monk, his eyes narrowing. "Sanctity is preserved by strength, venerable one. What good are prayers if the walls that protect them fall to ruin?"

The tension in the room crackled like a storm about to break. Kashyapa rose from his throne, his movements deliberate. The court fell silent, all eyes on their king.

"Enough," Kashyapa said, his voice commanding but calm. "The decision is mine, and it is final. Sigiriya will be our new capital. Rajith, you will oversee its transformation."

He turned to Sanghamitta, his gaze unwavering. "Your concerns are noted, Thera. But a king must think not only of faith but of survival. Sigiriya will be a beacon of both."

The monk's face darkened, but he bowed his head, his disapproval unspoken but palpable.

# CHAPTER 3: THE SACRED LAND

The path to Sigiriya wound through dense jungle, a labyrinth of towering trees and tangled vines that seemed to whisper with secrets of the ancient land. Kashyapa rode at the front of the procession, his mount's hooves crunching the undergrowth as the first rays of dawn pierced the canopy. Behind him, Rajith carried his leather satchel of sketches and tools, his sharp eyes scanning the surroundings with a mix of wonder and purpose. The air was thick with humidity, carrying the scent of earth and unseen blossoms, but it was the silence that unsettled them most. Birds and insects seemed to hold their tongues, as if the forest itself was in reverence or fear.

When they emerged into the clearing, Sigiriya rose before them, a colossal monolith of crimson stone that jutted out of the earth like a divine edict. Its surface was weathered by time, its cliffs sheer and unyielding, but it stood proud, unbroken by the centuries that had passed. Kashyapa halted his horse, staring at the rock in awe. For a moment, he felt small, a mere speck before the grandeur of nature's design.

"This is where it will begin," he murmured, his voice almost lost in the vastness of the clearing. "This is where we will reshape the destiny of Lanka."

Rajith dismounted, his gaze fixed on the rock with a fervor that bordered on obsession. "Your Majesty," he said, his voice reverent, "Sigiriya is a gift from the gods. Its height, its solitude —it is as if it was waiting for you."

Kashyapa nodded, but his eyes narrowed as he noticed something carved into the base of the rock. He dismounted and approached, his boots sinking slightly into the damp earth. The carving was faded, worn by time, but its shape was unmistakable: a serpent coiled around a lotus, its fangs bared in warning.

"What do you make of this?" Kashyapa asked, his voice tinged with curiosity.

Rajith joined him, kneeling to inspect the carving. His fingers traced the lines with care. "An ancient symbol," he said. "The serpent often represents protection in our myths, but it can also signify a curse. The lotus... purity, enlightenment. A strange pairing."

Kashyapa frowned, his unease growing. "A warning, perhaps?"

Rajith stood, brushing dirt from his hands. "Or a promise. It depends on how one chooses to see it."

---

The workers arrived the following day, their carts laden with tools and supplies. They moved cautiously, their eyes darting to the rock and the jungle beyond as if expecting something to emerge from the shadows. The first task was clearing the base, and as the workers hacked away at the undergrowth, they uncovered more carvings, each more intricate and unsettling than the last. Figures of half-human, half-animal forms danced across the stone, their eyes seeming to follow those who looked too closely.

Rumors began to spread among the laborers. Some claimed to hear voices at night, whispers carried on the wind that spoke in a language no one recognized. Others swore they saw figures moving among the trees, shadows that disappeared the moment they turned to look.

Kashyapa dismissed the reports at first, attributing them to the superstitions of simple men. But as the days passed, even he could not ignore the growing sense of unease. One evening, as he stood at the edge of the clearing, watching the sunset paint the rock in hues of fire, he felt a presence behind him.

"Your Majesty."

He turned to see a woman emerging from the jungle, her figure draped in a robe that shimmered like water in the fading light. Her face was striking, with eyes that seemed to pierce through him and a smile that was both serene and unsettling.

"Who are you?" Kashyapa demanded, his hand instinctively moving to the hilt of his sword.

The woman bowed her head slightly. "I am Varuni," she said, her voice as soft as the wind rustling through the leaves. "A seer who has come to aid you in your great endeavor."

Kashyapa studied her, his instincts torn between curiosity and caution. "Aid me? How?"

Varuni stepped closer, her movements graceful and deliberate. "I have seen what lies ahead, Your Majesty," she said. "Your rise and your fall. Sigiriya will be your legacy, but it will also be your trial. The path you have chosen is both glorious and perilous."

Kashyapa's eyes narrowed. "You speak in riddles, woman. If you have something to say, say it plainly."

Varuni's smile widened slightly, and she gestured toward the rock. "Sigiriya is not just stone and earth. It is alive, in ways you cannot yet understand. To claim it, you must first earn its favor. But beware, for it does not take kindly to those who come with pride in their hearts."

Rajith, who had joined them unnoticed, scoffed. "More superstition," he said, his tone dismissive. "Sigiriya is stone, nothing more. A blank canvas for the vision of a king."

Varuni's gaze shifted to the architect, her eyes narrowing. "Even stone remembers, Rajith. And this stone has a long memory."

In the days that followed, Varuni became a fixture at the site. She spoke little, but her presence was felt everywhere. Workers whispered about her, some calling her a witch, others a blessing. Kashyapa found himself drawn to her, despite his reservations. There was something about her—an air of certainty that both intrigued and unsettled him.

One night, unable to sleep, Kashyapa sought her out. He found her standing at the base of the rock, her hands resting lightly on its surface as if she could feel its pulse.

"What do you see?" he asked, his voice low.

Varuni did not turn. "I see a king who has claimed a throne but not yet his destiny," she said. "I see a fortress that will rise to touch the heavens, and a shadow that will grow to consume it."

Kashyapa stepped closer, his frustration bubbling to the surface. "Enough of your cryptic words," he said. "Tell me what I must do to ensure that my legacy endures."

Varuni turned to him then, her eyes gleaming in the moonlight. "You must listen," she said simply. "Listen to the rock, to the wind, to the whispers of those who came before. They will guide you, if you are willing to hear."

As the construction progressed, the whispers grew louder. One morning, as the workers began carving the first steps into the rock, they unearthed a chamber hidden within its base. The air that escaped was cold and stale, carrying with it the faint scent of decay. Inside, they found bones, ancient and brittle, arranged in a circle around a small stone altar.

Rajith examined the chamber with fascination, his fingers tracing the markings on the walls. "This is a burial site," he said. "Older than any we have found before. Perhaps the people who lived here worshipped the rock as a deity."

Varuni, who had been silent until now, stepped forward. "They did not worship it," she said. "They feared it."

Her words sent a ripple of unease through the group. Kashyapa said nothing, his mind racing. He could feel the weight of the rock pressing down on him, its presence as oppressive as it was magnificent. For the first time, he wondered if he had made a mistake.

But the thought was fleeting, banished by the force of his ambition. He turned to his men, his voice steady. "Seal the chamber," he commanded. "We have no need for the relics of the past. Our focus is on the future."

As the workers moved to obey, Varuni watched him with an inscrutable expression. "The past does not die so easily, Your Majesty," she said. "It lingers, waiting for the right moment to return."

Kashyapa met her gaze, his resolve unshaken. "Let it try," he said. "I will not be undone by ghosts."

Varuni's smile returned, faint and knowing. "We shall see," she said.

# CHAPTER 4:
# THE CURSE OF
# DHATUSENA

The moon hung low over Sigiriya, its pale light casting the rock in a ghostly glow. Kashyapa stood at the edge of the clearing, his silhouette framed by the fortress's looming shadow. The night was unnervingly quiet, save for the occasional rustle of leaves stirred by a phantom wind. In the stillness, Kashyapa felt the weight of his choices bearing down on him. The whispers of his father's final words returned to him, unbidden and relentless: The stones will remember this. So will the people.

Sleep had eluded him for days. When it finally came, it offered no solace. His dreams were plagued by visions of Dhatusena, his father's eyes blazing with reproach as he stood encased in the wall where he had been entombed. Kashyapa saw himself reaching out, only for Dhatusena to whisper, *You are cursed, my son,* before the stones swallowed him whole.

Kashyapa awoke with a start, the echo of his father's voice lingering in the oppressive darkness of his chambers. Sweat clung to his skin, and the faint aroma of incense did little to calm his racing heart. He rose and moved to the open balcony, the cool night air a small reprieve. Below, the flickering torchlights of the workers' camp dotted the landscape, a fragile semblance of order amidst the chaos.

---

The following morning, Kashyapa summoned Varuni to his chambers. The mystic entered without hesitation, her presence as unsettling as ever. Her dark eyes studied him intently, as if she already knew the nature of his summons.

"You have not slept," Varuni said, her tone matter-of-fact.

Kashyapa's jaw tightened. "My dreams are haunted," he admitted, his voice low. "My father... he accuses me, over and over, of betrayal. Even in death, he finds ways to torment me."

Varuni tilted her head slightly, her expression unreadable. "Dreams are often the whispers of the spirit world," she said. "Your father's soul is restless, bound to the mortal plane by the manner of his death."

Kashyapa's eyes narrowed. "You told me he was weak," he said, his voice edged with anger. "That his death was necessary for the strength of the kingdom."

"And so it was," Varuni replied calmly. "But necessity does not silence the echoes of injustice. The rock remembers, and so does your father."

Kashyapa turned away, his hands gripping the stone railing of the balcony. Below, the laborers toiled under the sun, their movements mechanical and uninspired. "What must I do?" he asked finally, his voice barely audible.

Varuni stepped closer, her presence a shadow that seemed to envelop him. "Appease the spirit of the rock," she said. "Perform the rites of purification and sacrifice. Only then can you hope to silence the voices that haunt you."

Kashyapa's stomach churned at the thought, but he nodded. "Very well. Prepare what is needed."

---

The preparations for the ritual began that evening. Varuni

directed the workers with precision, gathering herbs, oils, and symbols of spiritual significance. A circle was marked at the base of the rock, its boundaries etched with ancient runes that seemed to pulse faintly in the fading light. A sense of unease settled over the camp as the laborers watched the proceedings from a distance, their whispers carrying tales of curses and spirits.

As night fell, Kashyapa stood within the circle, his bare feet brushing against the cold earth. Varuni moved around him, chanting in a language he did not recognize. The air grew heavy, and the flames of the surrounding torches flickered as if caught in an unseen wind.

When the ritual ended, Varuni placed a small clay vessel at the center of the circle. "Leave this undisturbed," she instructed. "It will absorb the restless energy of the rock. In time, the whispers will fade."

Kashyapa nodded, though doubt lingered in his mind. He returned to his chambers, the weight of the ritual pressing against his thoughts. That night, his dreams were mercifully free of his father's specter, though an uneasy silence filled the void.

The following days brought a fragile calm to the camp. The workers' fears seemed to abate, and progress on the fortress resumed. But the reprieve was short-lived. One afternoon, a piercing scream shattered the air, drawing Kashyapa and his guards to the edge of the construction site.

A worker lay crumpled at the base of the rock, his body twisted at unnatural angles. Blood pooled beneath him, staining the earth. The man had been working on the upper scaffolding when he fell, but none could explain how or why. Some claimed they saw him reach out, as if grasping at an unseen force, before plummeting to his death.

"It is the curse," one of the workers whispered, his voice

trembling. "The rock does not want us here."

The murmur spread quickly, infecting the laborers like a plague. Kashyapa felt the tension rise, a palpable force that threatened to unravel all he had worked to build.

Varuni appeared at his side, her expression grim. "This is no accident," she said quietly. "The spirit of the rock is testing you, Your Majesty. It will not be satisfied with half measures."

Kashyapa turned to her, his frustration boiling over. "And what would you have me do?" he demanded. "How many more rituals must I perform? How much blood must be spilled?"

Varuni's gaze was steady, unyielding. "The rock requires devotion," she said. "True devotion. Only then will it accept you as its master."

Kashyapa's fists clenched, his mind racing. The weight of his ambition pressed against him, a relentless force that demanded he push forward, no matter the cost. He turned back to the rock, its crimson surface glowing faintly in the afternoon light.

"Then so be it," he said, his voice a whisper. "I will not be defeated by stone or shadow."

---

That night, as the camp settled into an uneasy stillness, Kashyapa stood alone before the rock. The moonlight bathed its surface, revealing the intricate carvings that had begun to emerge with the workers' efforts. He reached out, his fingers brushing against the cool stone, and for a moment, he thought he felt it pulse beneath his touch, as if alive.

"You will yield to me," he murmured, his voice firm. "You will become my legacy."

The wind picked up, carrying with it the faint sound of whispers. Kashyapa closed his eyes, letting the voices wash over him. They spoke of power and betrayal, of sacrifice and redemption. And as he stood there, alone in the shadow of the Lion Rock, Kashyapa felt the stirrings of something greater than himself—a force that promised both glory and ruin, if only he dared to claim it.

# CHAPTER 5: STRAINS IN THE COURT

The royal court of Anuradhapura was a kaleidoscope of tension and grandeur. Saffron-robed monks stood to one side, their serene faces betraying none of the turmoil brewing beneath their calm exteriors. On the opposite side, nobles in jewel-encrusted garments whispered among themselves, their voices barely audible over the low hum of political unease. Kashyapa, seated on the golden throne, surveyed them all with a measured gaze. The weight of his crown was matched only by the growing discontent that simmered beneath the surface.

The monks were the first to speak. Thera Sanghamitta, the eldest among them, stepped forward. His voice, though soft, carried the authority of centuries of tradition. "Your Majesty," he began, bowing slightly, "the constructions in Sigiriya have reached our ears. It is a matter of great concern to us and the faithful. The Lion Rock is sacred land, a place where our ancestors sought enlightenment. To transform it into a fortress is to defile its sanctity."

The court fell silent, all eyes on Kashyapa. The king leaned forward, his fingers drumming lightly on the armrest of his throne. "Thera," he said, his tone deceptively calm, "you speak of sanctity, but what sanctity is there in a city that cannot protect its people? Anuradhapura has been exposed to threats from within and without for too long. Sigiriya will be a fortress, yes, but it will also be a beacon—a testament to our strength and resilience."

Sanghamitta's expression darkened, but he held his tongue. Another monk stepped forward, his youthful face alight with indignation. "Strength without dharma is destruction, Your Majesty," he said, his voice trembling. "You risk inviting not only the wrath of the people but the wrath of the gods."

Murmurs rippled through the court. Kashyapa's eyes flashed with anger, but he forced himself to remain composed. "The gods," he said, his voice cold, "have little concern for mortal affairs. It is men who shape kingdoms, not divinities. And it is men who will build Sigiriya."

---

After the court adjourned, Commander Vihara approached Kashyapa in the privacy of the king's chambers. The commander's armor gleamed in the lamplight, but his expression was grave.

"Your Majesty," Vihara began, his tone cautious, "there are troubling signs among the army. Whispers of discontent are spreading. Some soldiers feel that abandoning Anuradhapura for Sigiriya is a betrayal of their heritage."

Kashyapa turned to face him, his jaw tightening. "And do you share their sentiment, Vihara?"

The commander hesitated, choosing his words carefully. "I serve the throne, not my personal opinions. But as your advisor, I must warn you—the more divided the army becomes, the weaker our defenses will be. And with Moggallana gathering strength in India, we cannot afford weakness."

The mention of Moggallana was like a blade to Kashyapa's pride. His half-brother had fled the kingdom after Dhatusena's death, vowing to return and reclaim what was rightfully his. The thought of Moggallana's forces marching on Sigiriya was a constant thorn in Kashyapa's mind, a shadow that darkened even his brightest visions.

"Moggallana is a coward," Kashyapa said, his voice sharp. "He hides in foreign lands, waiting for the day I falter. But he will not have that satisfaction. Sigiriya will be our strength, our shield. Let the soldiers grumble. Once they see what we have built, their doubts will vanish."

Vihara nodded, though his expression remained troubled. "As you command, Your Majesty."

Despite Kashyapa's confidence, the tensions within the court and the army continued to grow. The nobles, ever opportunistic, began aligning themselves with factions they believed would serve their interests best. Some supported Kashyapa's vision for Sigiriya, seeing it as a chance to secure their own legacies. Others whispered of Moggallana's potential return, their loyalty wavering as they weighed the odds.

Kashyapa was not blind to these machinations. He summoned his most trusted spies, instructing them to root out disloyalty and report back on the movements of the nobles. The web of intrigue that surrounded him grew thicker by the day, and with it, his paranoia.

One evening, as he paced the halls of his chambers, Varuni appeared, her arrival as silent as ever. She watched him for a moment before speaking.

"You are troubled," she said.

Kashyapa turned to her, his expression hard. "The court is filled with snakes," he said. "Even now, they plot against me, waiting for the moment I stumble."

Varuni stepped closer, her gaze piercing. "And do you trust me, Your Majesty?" she asked.

The question caught him off guard. He studied her face, searching for any hint of deceit. "You have proven your loyalty," he said carefully. "But trust is a luxury I cannot afford."

Varuni's lips curved into a faint smile. "Wise words," she said. "But wisdom alone will not protect you. You must act decisively, or the vipers in your midst will strike."

Kashyapa nodded, his resolve hardening. "Then I will strike first."

---

As the construction of Sigiriya progressed, Kashyapa's determination only grew stronger. The workers' efforts transformed the rock into a fortress of breathtaking complexity. Gardens began to take shape at its base, their design a testament to Rajith's genius. Intricate water systems were constructed, their channels flowing with precision. Kashyapa spent hours walking among the scaffolding, his eyes alight with the vision of what Sigiriya would become.

But even as the fortress rose, the weight of dissent pressed against him. One morning, a group of monks approached the construction site, their robes billowing in the wind. They stood in silent protest, their presence a stark reminder of the spiritual resistance to Kashyapa's plans.

The king descended from the scaffolding to meet them, his expression unreadable. "What is the meaning of this?" he demanded.

Thera Sanghamitta stepped forward, his gaze unwavering. "We come to remind you, Your Majesty, that the path you tread leads to ruin. This land is sacred. To defile it is to invite a curse upon yourself and your kingdom."

Kashyapa's eyes narrowed. "You speak of curses as if they are tangible threats," he said. "But curses are nothing compared to the blades of my enemies. Sigiriya will protect us from them. Can your prayers do the same?"

The monks remained silent, their stillness a quiet defiance. Kashyapa turned away, his frustration bubbling beneath the surface. As he ascended back to the scaffolding, he felt the weight of their gaze upon him, as if they were judging not just his actions but his soul.

---

That night, Kashyapa sat alone in his chambers, staring at a map of the kingdom. The lines and symbols blurred before his eyes, the weight of his decisions pressing against him. He thought of his father, entombed in the wall, and of Moggallana, waiting in the shadows. The whispers of the monks echoed in his mind, their warnings mingling with the doubts he fought to suppress.

A knock at the door drew him from his thoughts. It was Vihara, his expression grim.

"What is it?" Kashyapa asked.

"A message from the southern provinces," Vihara said, handing him a scroll. "There are rumors of rebellion. The nobles grow restless."

Kashyapa read the scroll in silence, his jaw tightening with each word. When he finished, he set it aside and rose to his feet.

"Let them grumble," he said. "Sigiriya will silence them all. Once it is complete, there will be no question of my power."

Vihara nodded, though his unease was clear. As he left, Kashyapa returned to the map, his thoughts a storm of ambition and fear. The path he had chosen was fraught with peril, but there was no turning back. Sigiriya would be his legacy, no matter the cost.

# CHAPTER 6: THE ARCHITECT'S OBSESSION

The Lion Rock had begun to transform. Scaffolding snaked up its sheer face, and the clang of hammers and chisels echoed through the jungle. Gardens took root at its base, the once-wild land sculpted into terraces that seemed to flow like the veins of the earth. Water channels gleamed under the sunlight, their precision an engineering marvel. For all its progress, however, Sigiriya seemed to loom larger and darker, a presence that both inspired awe and whispered unease.

At the center of this transformation was Rajith. The architect's obsession with the project had become all-consuming. Day and night, he moved through the site with feverish energy, his robes streaked with dust and sweat. His once-sharp features were now hollowed, his eyes blazing with an intensity that bordered on madness. To those who worked under him, he was both a visionary and a tyrant, driving them to match his impossible pace.

"This is not just a fortress," Rajith told Kashyapa during one of their rare moments of conversation. "It is a symbol. A monument to your reign, yes, but also a bridge between the mortal and the divine. When Sigiriya is complete, it will rival the heavens themselves."

Kashyapa's gaze lingered on the rock, his expression unreadable. He admired Rajith's fervor, but it also unnerved him. "Do not let ambition blind you," he said. "The gods do not take kindly to mortals who presume too much."

Rajith laughed, a sound devoid of humor. "The gods will have no choice but to acknowledge us," he said. "Sigiriya will demand it."

As the days turned into weeks, whispers of strange occurrences increased among the workers. Some spoke of eerie sounds— a low, rhythmic drumming that seemed to emanate from deep within the rock. Others claimed to see shadows moving where no one stood, dark shapes that flickered at the edge of their vision. The most unsettling rumors came from those who worked on the upper scaffolding. They swore they felt the rock tremble beneath their feet, as if it were alive and displeased.

Kashyapa dismissed the reports at first, attributing them to exhaustion and superstition. But when a laborer came to him directly, his face pale and his hands trembling, the king found himself unable to ignore the growing unease.

"Your Majesty," the man stammered, his voice thick with fear. "Something is wrong with this place. We hear... things. Voices that do not belong to any man. And last night, one of the stones moved on its own. We cannot explain it."

Kashyapa's expression hardened. "You are tired," he said. "Fear clouds your judgment. Return to your work, and speak no more of this."

The laborer hesitated, but the weight of Kashyapa's gaze silenced him. He bowed and retreated, though his fear remained palpable.

Rajith's response to the workers' fears was swift and unyielding. "They are cowards," he declared, his voice sharp with disdain.

"Do they think greatness comes without sacrifice? Let them whisper their nonsense. I will not let their fears slow us."

But as the incidents continued, Rajith's demeanor began to change. He grew more irritable, lashing out at workers who questioned him. He spent hours alone on the scaffolding, sketching designs and muttering to himself. One evening, Kashyapa found him standing at the highest point of the construction site, staring at the horizon with a faraway look in his eyes.

"Rajith," Kashyapa called, his voice cutting through the dusk. "What are you doing up here?"

Rajith turned slowly, his face gaunt and his eyes shadowed. "Listening," he said.

Kashyapa frowned. "Listening to what?"

Rajith gestured toward the rock. "To it. Sigiriya speaks, Your Majesty. It whispers of its purpose, of what it demands. Do you not hear it?"

Kashyapa's unease deepened. "You are overworked," he said. "Take a day to rest. Clear your mind."

Rajith shook his head, a faint smile tugging at his lips. "Rest? How can I rest when there is so much to do? Sigiriya must be perfect. Only then will it be satisfied."

---

Varuni watched Rajith's descent into obsession with quiet intensity. She approached Kashyapa one evening, her presence as unsettling as ever. "Your architect walks a dangerous path," she said. "His mind is unraveling, and the rock is feeding on it."

Kashyapa's frustration flared. "More riddles?" he snapped. "Speak plainly, Varuni."

She met his gaze, her eyes dark and unwavering. "Rajith's obsession binds him to it, but such bonds are rarely one-sided. If you do not intervene, he will destroy himself—and perhaps this kingdom with him."

Kashyapa considered her words, his mind racing. He thought of Rajith's brilliance, his tireless dedication, and the fortress that was taking shape under his guidance. Could he afford to lose such a man? And yet, could he afford to keep him?

The breaking point came during a storm. Thunder rolled across the jungle, and rain lashed against the scaffolding. Workers scrambled to secure the construction site, their shouts barely audible over the howling wind. Kashyapa stood in his chambers, watching the chaos unfold through the open balcony doors.

A messenger arrived, drenched and breathless. "Your Majesty," he said, "Rajith... he is still on the rock. He refuses to come down."

Kashyapa's eyes widened. Without hesitation, he donned his cloak and made his way to the site, his guards following close behind. The rain soaked through his robes as he climbed the slippery paths to the scaffolding. When he reached the upper levels, he found Rajith standing on an unfinished platform, his arms outstretched as if embracing the storm.

"Rajith!" Kashyapa shouted over the wind. "Get down at once!"

The architect turned, his face illuminated by a flash of lightning. There was a wildness in his eyes, a fervor that sent a chill down Kashyapa's spine. "Do you see it, Your Majesty?" Rajith cried, his voice exultant. "Do you see what we are creating? Sigiriya will be eternal, a beacon that defies the gods themselves!"

"You will die if you stay up here!" Kashyapa warned, stepping closer. "Come down, and we will speak of this in the morning."

Rajith laughed, a sound that was both joyous and unhinged. "Death?" he said. "Death is nothing compared to this. Sigiriya is worth any sacrifice."

A sudden gust of wind rocked the platform, and Kashyapa lunged forward, grabbing Rajith's arm. For a moment, their eyes met, and Kashyapa saw the depths of Rajith's madness. Then, with a strength that defied his gaunt frame, Rajith pulled free and stepped backward, his foot slipping on the wet wood.

Kashyapa reached out, but it was too late. Rajith fell, his scream was swallowed by the storm. The sound of his body hitting the rocks below was drowned out by a crack of thunder.

---

The storm subsided by morning, leaving the camp in a state of shock. Rajith's body was retrieved and buried near the base of Sigiriya, his grave marked by a simple stone. The workers whispered of curses and sacrifices; their fears reignited by the architect's tragic end.

Kashyapa stood at the grave; his expression grim. Varuni appeared beside him; her presence as silent as ever.

"He gave everything for this," Kashyapa said, his voice heavy with both admiration and regret.

"And Sigiriya took it," Varuni replied. "The rock is not yet satisfied, Your Majesty. It will demand more before it is complete."

Kashyapa's jaw tightened, his resolve hardening. "Then it will have more," he said. "Sigiriya will be finished, no matter the cost."

# CHAPTER 7:
# THE RITUAL

The air around Sigiriya hung heavy with an unnatural stillness, the kind that precedes a storm. Yet, no clouds darkened the horizon, and no winds disturbed the jungle canopy. The workers moved about their tasks in hushed tones, their usual banter replaced by an oppressive quiet. Even the birds, which had once filled the air with their calls, seemed to have fled. Kashyapa stood at the edge of the construction site, his gaze fixed on the towering rock that seemed to watch him in return.

Varuni's voice broke the silence. "The time has come, Your Majesty."

He turned to face her. She stood barefoot, her flowing robes adorned with symbols that seemed to shift and shimmer in the waning light. In her hands, she held a bowl carved from obsidian, its surface etched with runes that pulsed faintly.

"The rock demands acknowledgment," she said, her tone both solemn and urgent. "A ritual of appeasement must be performed. Only then will Sigiriya yield to your will."

Kashyapa's jaw tightened. He had never been one to place faith in mysticism, but the events of recent weeks had shaken his skepticism. The whispers, the shadows, and the mysterious disturbances around the site—all pointed to forces beyond his understanding. If this ritual could quell the unease that gripped the camp, then so be it.

"What must I do?" he asked, his voice steady.

Varuni smiled faintly, a flicker of approval crossing her face. "Follow me."

---

The ritual site was prepared at the base of the rock, where an ancient carving of a serpent coiled around a lotus had been uncovered weeks earlier. A circle had been drawn around the carving, its boundaries marked with symbols painted in blood-red dye. Torches surrounded the area, their flames flickering against the encroaching darkness.

Kashyapa stepped into the circle, his bare feet brushing against the cool earth. The gathered workers and guards watched from a distance, their faces etched with a mixture of fear and curiosity. Varuni stood at the edge of the circle, chanting in a language that seemed older than the rock itself. Her voice rose and fell like the rhythm of waves, weaving a melody that sent shivers down Kashyapa's spine.

She handed him the obsidian bowl, which now held a mixture of water, herbs, and a single crimson drop that Kashyapa knew to be blood. "Pour this over the carving," she instructed. "As you do, speak these words." She leaned in close, whispering an incantation into his ear. The words felt strange and heavy on his tongue, as if they carried a weight beyond their sound.

Kashyapa hesitated for a moment, then stepped forward. The carving seemed to glow faintly in the torchlight, its serpent's eyes glinting as if alive. He poured the contents of the bowl over it, the liquid gliding along the grooves of the carving like veins filling with blood.

"I offer this as tribute," Kashyapa said, his voice firm despite the unease coiling in his stomach. "May the spirit of Sigiriya guide and protect this endeavor."

As the last of the liquid disappeared into the earth, a sudden gust of wind extinguished the torches. The crowd gasped, their whispers rising like the rustling of leaves. For a moment, darkness enveloped the site, and the air seemed to hum with energy. Then, as quickly as it had come, the wind stilled, and the torches reignited, their flames burning brighter than before.

Varuni's voice rang out, clear and triumphant. "The rock has accepted your offering, Your Majesty. Its power is now bound to you."

---

The ritual seemed to have an immediate effect on the camp. The workers' fears began to abate, their whispers replaced by renewed focus. Even the jungle, which had felt so foreboding, seemed to relax, its sounds returning in a tentative symphony. Kashyapa felt a strange calm settled over him, as if a great weight had been lifted from his shoulders.

But the calm was deceptive. Kashyapa had performed another ritual weeks earlier, a desperate act to ward off the recurring nightmares of his father's judgment. In those dreams, Dhatusena's spectral form accused him of betrayal, his voice echoing with condemnation. That earlier ritual—a solitary act— had demanded a personal price: a drop of his own blood. It had silenced the dreams temporarily but left a lingering dread in its wake. He wondered if this new ritual would truly end the unrest or merely delay the inevitable reckoning.

Rajith, the brilliant architect who had once stood beside Kashyapa, was no longer alive to voice his concerns. His death, shrouded in mystery, had already cast a pall over Sigiriya's construction. The whispers in the camp hinted at curses and vengeance, though Kashyapa had long stopped entertaining such thoughts. Rajith's legacy lay in the half-finished walls and intricate designs—a testament to his unmatched genius. Yet Kashyapa could not shake the feeling that Rajith's absence had left an unfillable void, one that the ritual's outcome could not mend.

That night, Kashyapa dreamed again. He stood at Sigiriya's summit, the world spread out before him in a sea of green and gold. The fortress was complete, its walls gleaming in the sunlight, its gardens teeming with life. But as he gazed upon his creation, the ground beneath his feet began to tremble. Cracks snaked through the stone, and a deep, resonant voice echoed in his mind: You have taken much. Now you must give.

He woke with a start, the words still ringing in his ears. The calm he had felt after the ritual was gone, replaced by a gnawing sense of foreboding. He rose and stepped out onto the balcony, the cool night air doing little to soothe his unease. Below, the torches of the workers' camp flickered like stars, a fragile light against the encroaching darkness.

Varuni appeared beside him, her arrival as silent as always. "You are troubled," she said, her voice soft.

Kashyapa did not look at her. "The rock accepted the offering. Yet I feel... restless. As if it demands more."

Varuni's eyes gleamed in the moonlight. "Sigiriya will test you, push you to your limits. But it is through these trials that you will achieve greatness. Do not falter now."

Kashyapa turned to her, his gaze piercing. "And if the rock's demands become too great?"

Varuni smiled faintly, a knowing look in her eyes. "Greatness always comes at a price."

# CHAPTER 8: AHALYA'S CHRONICLE

The golden glow of dawn filtered through the lattice windows of the palace, casting intricate patterns on the cool stone walls. Ahalya sat at her writing desk, the faint scratching of her quill the only sound in the quiet chamber. Scrolls and parchment lay scattered around her, a chaotic testament to her efforts to document Kashyapa's reign. She had been tasked with recording the king's ambitions and achievements, but the task had grown more complex than she had ever anticipated.

Her writings began as a chronicle of glory: Kashyapa's bold vision for Sigiriya, his determination to reshape the kingdom, and the grandiose projects that were taking form under his rule. Yet, as the weeks turned into months, her chronicles took on darker tones. The fractures within the court, the whispers of curses, and the ominous events surrounding the construction of Sigiriya seeped into her narrative. She found herself not merely documenting history but piecing together a puzzle of intrigue and foreboding.

Ahalya's role within the court was unique. As a scribe, she was privy to conversations and decisions that others were not. She moved silently through the palace halls, her presence often overlooked, yet her sharp mind absorbed everything. It was during one such unassuming moment that she overheard a conversation between two nobles in a dimly lit corridor.

"Dhatusena's death still haunts this court," one whispered, his voice barely audible.

"Haunts? It's a festering wound," the other replied. "And not just because of the king's ghost. Do you truly believe Kashyapa acted alone?"

Ahalya froze, her quill hovering over a blank scroll as she strained to hear more. The nobles' voices dropped further, and she could only catch fragments of their conversation: "manipulated... whispers in his ear... the nobles have more power than the king knows."

Her heart raced as she retreated to her chamber, the weight of their words pressing against her thoughts. Could it be true? Had Kashyapa been a pawn in a larger game, his actions driven by forces beyond his control? The possibility reframed everything she had written so far, casting a shadow over the narrative of his ambition.

---

That evening, Ahalya sought answers the only way she knew by diving into the archives. The palace's library was a vast and dimly lit chamber, its shelves lined with records that spanned generations. She poured over documents detailing Dhatusena's reign, treaties signed, alliances forged, and court proceedings. Among them, she found veiled references to dissent within the noble class, subtle but undeniable hints of unrest that predated Kashyapa's coup.

Her search also led her to the writings of Dhatusena himself. In a faded journal, she discovered entries that spoke of distrust toward his council, warnings of treachery that seemed to echo through the pages. One entry, in particular, stood out: *The lion's den is full of vipers. I can trust no one but my blood, and even that is uncertain.*

The words chilled her. Had Dhatusena foreseen his downfall? And if so, had Kashyapa acted out of ambition alone, or had he been manipulated by those who stood to gain the most from his rise?

---

Ahalya's discoveries weighed heavily on her. She could not confront Kashyapa directly; her position in the court was tenuous at best, and the king's temper had grown unpredictable. Yet she felt compelled to act, to unravel the truth behind the conspiracy that seemed to coil around the throne like a serpent.

Her chance came during a rare moment of candor with Varuni. The mystic had taken an interest in Ahalya's chronicles, often appearing unannounced to read over her shoulder or offer cryptic commentary. On this occasion, Ahalya decided to test Varuni's knowledge.

"Do you believe the king acted alone?" Ahalya asked, keeping her tone neutral.

Varuni looked up from the scroll she had been perusing, her dark eyes unreadable. "Alone?" she echoed. "No king acts alone. The throne is both a shield and a shackle, and those who sit upon it are never free of influence."

Ahalya pressed on, her pulse quickening. "But could he have been... misled? By those who sought to use him for their own ends?"

For a moment, Varuni said nothing. Then she leaned closer, her voice dropping to a whisper. "Kashyapa's ambition is his own, but ambition is a flame that others will feed if it suits their purpose. The nobles, the council, even the spirits of this land—all have their agendas. Be careful where your questions lead you, Ahalya. The answers may not be what you hope to find."

---

The next day, Ahalya's suspicions deepened when she observed a meeting between Kashyapa and his council. The nobles' deference to the king seemed forced, their smiles thin and their words laced with subtle barbs. One noble, a portly man named Sena, spoke with exaggerated enthusiasm about the progress at Sigiriya.

"A marvel of our time, Your Majesty," Sena declared. "The people will speak of your greatness for generations to come."

Kashyapa's expression was unreadable, but Ahalya noticed the flicker of doubt in his eyes. He thanked Sena curtly and moved on, but the exchange lingered in her mind. Sena's tone had been too eager, his praise too calculated. It was as if he were trying to placate a beast, he feared might turn on him.

That night, Ahalya began a new chapter in her chronicles, one she titled "The Veil of Power." She wrote of the cracks forming in Kashyapa's court, the whispers of conspiracy, and the lingering question of Dhatusena's death. Her quill moved swiftly, the words pouring out as if compelled by a force beyond herself.

As she wrote, a strange sensation crept over her. The room seemed to grow colder, the shadows in the corners stretching and deepening. She paused, glancing over her shoulder, but the chamber was empty. Shaking off the feeling, she returned to her work, determined to document the truth, no matter the cost.

Her final lines for the night were a warning, not just to future readers but to herself: *In the pursuit of power, truth is often the first casualty. But even buried, it leaves traces, waiting for the moment it will rise again.*

Unbeknownst to Ahalya, her writings were not as private as she believed. The next morning, a pair of eyes lingered on the parchment she had left on her desk. The figure's hand hovered over the scroll, fingers brushing the edges before retreating into the shadows.

The court's secrets were many, and Ahalya was not the only one seeking to uncover them.

# CHAPTER 9: THE ARCHITECT'S DEFIANCE

The morning sun bathed Sigiriya in a golden light, illuminating the fortress as it rose from the jungle like an edict of power. The progress was undeniable; terraces of lush gardens now cascaded along the rock's base, while intricate waterways sparkled with precision. Yet within this beauty, tension festered like an unseen wound.

Rajith had been replaced.

Months earlier, Rajith's death had sent shock waves through the court, and whispers of curses and betrayal lingered like an unwelcome shadow. The burden of finishing the ambitious project now fell to Darshana, a young and untested architect thrust into a role that demanded both genius and fortitude.

Darshana stood atop the scaffolding, squinting against the sun as he reviewed the latest changes Kashyapa had demanded. The king's insistence on thicker walls, additional watchtowers, and strategic battlements had thrown the existing designs into chaos. To Darshana, these changes felt like a desperate attempt to fortify against an unseen enemy—or perhaps, the king's own paranoia.

"You cannot simply carve majesty from the rock and then shackle it with fear," Darshana muttered under his breath. He clutched the amended plans, his fingers tightening around the parchment as frustration simmered beneath his calm exterior.

Footsteps approached, and Darshana turned to see Kashyapa ascending the scaffolding with the ease of a man who belonged above the world. Flanked by two guards, the king's presence was commanding, his gaze sharp and assessing.

"Darshana," Kashyapa said, his voice carrying the weight of authority. "Have the adjustments been made?"

Darshana held up the plans, his voice steady but edged with restraint. "Your Majesty, these changes... they disrupt the harmony of the design. Sigiriya is meant to inspire awe, not dread. These fortifications risk undermining its very essence."

Kashyapa's expression darkened, a flicker of impatience crossing his face. "Sigiriya is meant to endure," he replied. "It must stand as an unbreachable fortress, a testament to power and resilience. Beauty alone will not shield us from Moggallana's forces."

Darshana's jaw tightened, but he met the king's gaze. "Endurance does not come from walls alone, Your Majesty. It comes from the vision that shapes them. What you ask... it changes Sigiriya from a symbol of unity to one of fear."

The tension crackled between them, the air thick with unspoken defiance. Kashyapa's voice lowered, his tone icy. "You tread dangerously close to the path that doomed Rajith. Do not make me question your loyalty, Darshana."

The young architect's resolve faltered, and he bowed his head. "As you command, Your Majesty."

---

That evening, Darshana retreated to his quarters, his thoughts a storm of frustration and doubt. The plans lay scattered across his desk, their once-precise lines marred by hastily scribbled corrections. He stared at them, the weight of his role pressing heavily on his shoulders.

The sound of a knock at the door pulled him from his thoughts. When he opened it, Varuni stood in the doorway, her presence as unsettling as it was enigmatic. She stepped inside without waiting for an invitation, her eyes scanning the room with an almost predatory curiosity.

"You seem troubled, Darshana," she said, her voice soft but laced with an unnerving certainty.

Darshana gestured to the plans, his frustration bubbling over. "Look at this," he said bitterly. "Sigiriya was meant to be a masterpiece, a beacon of greatness. Now it's becoming a prison of stone and paranoia."

Varuni's gaze lingered on the plans before shifting to the young architect. "And yet, even prisons can serve a purpose," she said. "Perhaps the changes are not a betrayal, but an evolution. The question is not what is being lost, but what will endure."

Darshana shook his head, his voice rising with emotion. "You speak in riddles, Varuni. Do you not see what's at stake? If this continues, Sigiriya will be remembered not for its splendor, but for the fear that built it."

Varuni stepped closer, her gaze piercing. "Fear and splendor are often two sides of the same coin," she said. "The king's vision is driven by forces you cannot begin to understand. You must decide where your loyalty lies—with the king, or with the rock."

Her words hung in the air long after she left, leaving Darshana to grapple with the weight of her cryptic counsel.

---

Kashyapa walked the grounds of Sigiriya that night, the shadows stretching long and jagged under the pale light of the moon. His thoughts turned to the ritual he had performed weeks earlier, a desperate attempt to silence the haunting dreams of his father. The blood offering to the serpent carved into the rock had quelled the nightmares, but it had not eased the growing unease within him.

As he approached the site of the ritual, the air grew colder, the silence oppressive. The serpent's carved eyes seemed to glint with a faint, otherworldly light. Kashyapa hesitated, his breath visible in the chill night air.

"I have done what was required," he murmured, his voice barely audible. "Why does the unrest persist?"

The rock seemed to whisper in response, the sound faint and indistinct. Kashyapa stepped back, a shiver running through him. The ritual had silenced his father's voice, but now it seemed the rock itself had begun to speak. Whether it was a warning or an omen, he could not say.

---

The next day, a council meeting was called. The nobles gathered in the grand hall, their faces a mixture of apprehension and curiosity. Kashyapa took his place at the head of the table, his demeanor as commanding as ever but with an undercurrent of strain that did not go unnoticed.

Darshana entered the hall, his movements deliberate, his expression composed despite the turmoil within him. He carried the latest plans, their edges worn from endless revisions.

"Darshana," Kashyapa began, his tone sharp. "Explain to the council why the latest fortifications remain incomplete."

The architect stepped forward, his voice steady but firm. "Your Majesty, the changes you have ordered compromise the structural integrity of the design. Implementing them could weaken the foundation."

A murmur spread through the council, the nobles exchanging wary glances. Kashyapa's eyes narrowed, his voice cutting through the whispers. "Do not insult my intelligence, Darshana. You resist not out of concern for the foundation, but because you lack the resolve to see this vision through."

Darshana's composure wavered, but he held his ground. "I resist because I believe in what Sigiriya was meant to represent," he said. "A symbol of unity, not a fortress of fear."

The tension in the room was palpable, the air thick with the weight of unspoken challenges. Kashyapa's voice dropped, his tone dangerous. "You forget your place, Darshana. Sigiriya is not yours to define. It is mine."

The young architect bowed his head, his voice subdued. "As you command, Your Majesty."

---

That night, the winds howled around Sigiriya, their mournful cries echoing through the jungle. Darshana sat alone in his quarters, the candlelight casting flickering shadows on the walls. He stared at the plans before him, Varuni's words echoing in his mind: *You must decide where your loyalty lies—with the king, or with the rock.*

As the candle burned low, Darshana made his decision. But whether it would lead to redemption or ruin remained to be seen.

# CHAPTER 10: SHADOWS OF TRUST

The nights at Sigiriya had grown colder, the winds slicing through the jungle and carrying whispers that seemed to come from the rock itself. Kashyapa stood on the highest terrace, his silhouette illuminated by the silver moonlight. Below, the fortress buzzed with activity, even at this late hour. Workers moved about like shadows, their movements hurried, their voices low. It was as if the entire camp sensed the growing tension, a storm building in the king's court.

Varuni appeared beside him, her arrival silent as always. She wore a cloak that billowed in the wind, and her dark eyes gleamed with a knowing light.

"Your Majesty," she began, her voice soft but firm. "The rock speaks of betrayal."

Kashyapa turned to her, his face a mask of exhaustion and suspicion. "Betrayal?" he repeated. "From whom?"

Varuni tilted her head, her expression unreadable. "The signs are unclear, but the danger is close. Closer than you realize."

Kashyapa's mind raced. Over the past weeks, he had sensed the unease spreading among his court and workers. Whispers of dissent, secretive glances, and the subtle changes in Darshana, the new architect, all pointed to fractures within his kingdom.

"What do you suggest?" Kashyapa asked.

Varuni's gaze sharpened. "Watch them, Your Majesty. All of them. The court, the nobles, the workers. Even those you trust most."

---

The following morning, Kashyapa summoned his closest guards and issued new orders. Spies were placed among the workers, tasked with listening for rumors and uncovering any signs of conspiracy. Courtiers found their movements quietly monitored, their correspondence intercepted. Even the king's inner circle was not spared scrutiny.

Kashyapa himself began visiting the construction site more frequently, questioning workers about their progress and their loyalties. Though his tone was calm, the intensity of his gaze left many uneasy. The workers' whispers shifted from fears of curses to fears of the king himself.

One evening, Kashyapa's attention turned to Darshana. The young architect had taken over after Rajith's demise, and while his designs were precise and efficient, they lacked the spiritual connection that Rajith had brought to the project. Kashyapa wondered if Darshana's pragmatic approach masked deeper ambitions.

"Darshana seems loyal enough," Commander Vihara told Kashyapa during a private meeting. "But there are murmurs among the workers. They say he's too focused on speed, cutting corners to meet deadlines. Some even claim he's hiding something."

Kashyapa frowned. "Hiding what?"

Vihara hesitated. "I don't know, Your Majesty. But I've seen him lingering in the southern chambers, places that were Rajith's domain before his... passing."

The king's gaze darkened. "Then I will see for myself."

---

That night, Kashyapa visited Darshana's quarters unannounced.

He found the architect hunched over a table, surrounded by sketches and fragments of stone. The room was dimly lit, the flickering candlelight casting eerie shadows on the walls.

"Darshana," Kashyapa said, his voice cutting through the silence. "We need to talk."

Darshana looked up, his expression tense but composed. "Your Majesty," he said, rising to his feet. "To what do I owe this honor?"

Kashyapa stepped closer, his gaze sweeping over the disarray. "There are rumors," he said. "Whispers of secrecy and dissent. Workers disappearing, restricted areas. What are you hiding?"

Darshana's jaw tightened. "I hide nothing," he said evenly. "My only loyalty is to Sigiriya. Everything I do is for its completion."

"Then why the secrecy?" Kashyapa demanded. "Why consort with workers in areas I have not authorized?"

Darshana's composure faltered. "Your Majesty, those areas were Rajith's domain," he said. "I was only trying to understand his designs, to ensure continuity. The workers who assisted me… they feared your wrath if they spoke out of turn."

The mention of Rajith stirred an old wound in Kashyapa. The ritual he had performed to silence his father's dreams still weighed heavily on his soul. Rajith's death, though justified in his mind, had left the project haunted by whispers and doubts.

"Be careful, Darshana," Kashyapa said coldly. "Your loyalty is under question. Do not give me reason to doubt you further."

---

Over the next few days, the atmosphere at Sigiriya grew increasingly tense. Kashyapa's spies reported little of substance, but their presence only fueled the workers' unease. Darshana, though outwardly cooperative, seemed more withdrawn, his movements careful and measured.

One afternoon, a worker approached Kashyapa directly. The man's face was pale, his voice trembling. "Your Majesty," he said, bowing low. "There is something you must see."

Kashyapa followed the man to a secluded area near the base of the rock, where a hidden chamber had been unearthed. The air inside was cold and stale, and the walls were covered in carvings that seemed to writhe in the torchlight. At the center of the chamber stood an altar, its surface stained with dark, dried streaks.

"This... this is what Darshana has been studying," the worker whispered. "He comes here often, always alone. We dare not question him."

Kashyapa stared at the altar, his unease deepening. The carvings on the walls depicted scenes of sacrifice and power, their meaning obscure but undeniably sinister. He turned to the worker. "Say nothing of this to anyone," he ordered. "Return to your duties."

As the worker left, Kashyapa remained in the chamber, his mind racing. Was this proof of Darshana's betrayal, or something else entirely? The lines between loyalty and treachery, reality and myth, were blurring, and Kashyapa felt himself teetering on the edge of understanding.

---

That evening, Kashyapa confronted Varuni. The mystic listened silently as he described the hidden chamber, her expression unreadable.

"What does it mean?" Kashyapa demanded. "Is Darshana conspiring against me, or is this something... darker?"

Varuni's gaze was steady. "The rock tests all who seek to claim it," she said. "Darshana's actions may be his own, or they may be influenced by forces beyond our comprehension. Either way, the danger is real."

"What should I do?" Kashyapa asked, his voice tinged with desperation.

Varuni stepped closer, her voice dropping to a whisper. "Watch him closely, but do not act in haste. The truth will reveal itself in time, if you have the patience to see it."

Kashyapa nodded, though his resolve was far from certain. The shadows around him were growing darker, and the light of trust seemed increasingly out of reach.

# CHAPTER 11: THE BREAKING POINT

The air around Sigiriya was heavy, almost suffocating, as though the rock itself had absorbed the tension brewing within Kashyapa's court. Clouds gathered ominously above, casting shadows over the fortress's burgeoning walls. The workers moved with a subdued air, their usual banter replaced by silence, as if they too felt the weight of something unseen pressing down upon them.

Kashyapa strode through the construction site, his steps purposeful and his face a mask of barely contained fury. The hidden chamber, the strange altar, and the whispers of conspiracy all pointed to one man. Darshana. His once-brilliant architect had become an enigma, his every action cloaked in secrecy. Kashyapa's trust in him had eroded, replaced by a gnawing suspicion that grew with each passing day.

When Kashyapa entered Darshana's quarters unannounced, he found the architect hunched over a table, his fingers tracing designs etched into stone tablets. The room smelled of burnt herbs and something acrid that made Kashyapa's nose wrinkle. Darshana looked up, his eyes bloodshot and rimmed with dark circles. He seemed startled but quickly masked his surprise with a thin smile.

"Your Majesty," Darshana said, standing and bowing slightly. "To what do I owe this unexpected visit?"

Kashyapa stepped forward, his voice cold and measured. "Spare me the pleasantries. I know about the chamber. The altar. The carvings. What have you been doing, Darshana?"

Darshana's expression shifted, his smile fading. "I have been… studying," he said carefully. "Sigiriya is more than just stone and mortar. There are… forces at work here, forces that must be understood if we are to complete the project."

"Forces?" Kashyapa's voice rose, his anger bubbling to the surface. "You speak of forces, yet you conceal your actions, bar my men, and conduct rituals in secret. Do you take me for a fool?"

Darshana's jaw tightened. "You misunderstand, Your Majesty. Everything I do is for Sigiriya. The chamber, the altar—they are tools, not betrayals. The rock demands respect, and I am merely answering its call."

Kashyapa's fists clenched. "Respect?" he hissed. "Or collusion? Have you allied yourself with these so-called forces to undermine me?"

The accusation hung in the air like a dagger poised to strike. Darshana's eyes widened, and he stepped back, raising his hands defensively. "I would never betray you," he said, his voice trembling. "You must believe me."

But Kashyapa saw only defiance in Darshana's words, a challenge to his authority that he could not ignore. The weight of weeks—months—of paranoia and betrayal crashed over him like a wave, drowning all reason. Before he realized what he was doing, he lunged forward, his hands wrapping around Darshana's throat.

Darshana struggled, his hands clawing at Kashyapa's arms, but the king's grip was unrelenting. The room seemed to darken, the flickering candlelight casting grotesque shadows on the walls. Kashyapa's vision blurred, and all he could hear was the pounding of his own heart, drowning out Darshana's gasping pleas.

When it was over, Darshana's body slumped to the floor, lifeless. Kashyapa staggered back, his chest heaving as he stared down at the architect. The reality of what he had done began to sink in, but it brought no clarity, only a deeper sense of foreboding.

---

The guards who arrived moments later found Kashyapa standing over Darshana's body, his hands trembling and his face pale. They said nothing, their expressions carefully neutral as they awaited his command.

"Take him," Kashyapa said finally, his voice hollow. "Bury him in the foundations. Let his spirit bind this fortress together."

The guards hesitated for a moment but then obeyed, lifting Darshana's body and carrying it out of the quarters. Kashyapa watched them go, his mind a whirlwind of thoughts. He told himself that it had been necessary, that Darshana's betrayal had left him no choice. Yet a small voice within whispered otherwise, a voice he tried desperately to silence.

---

That night, Kashyapa sat alone in his chambers, staring into the flickering flames of a brazier. The firelight danced across the walls, casting shapes that seemed to move of their own accord. He closed his eyes, but the images of Darshana's lifeless face and the strange carvings in the hidden chamber refused to fade.

Varuni entered without knocking, her presence as unsettling as ever. She moved to stand beside him, her gaze fixed on the fire.

"It is done," she said quietly. "The rock has claimed its sacrifice."

Kashyapa's eyes snapped open, and he turned to her, his voice sharp. "You knew this would happen."

Varuni met his gaze, her expression calm. "I knew the rock would test you," she said. "And I knew you would rise to meet that test. Darshana's death was inevitable. His defiance threatened not just your vision but the very soul of Sigiriya."

"And what of my soul?" Kashyapa demanded. "How many more

must die before this fortress is complete?"

Varuni's eyes darkened. "Greatness always demands sacrifice," she said. "But it is not the deaths that weigh upon you, Your Majesty. It is your doubt. Embrace your destiny, and the whispers will cease."

Kashyapa turned back to the fire, his jaw tightening. "Leave me," he said.

Varuni hesitated, then bowed and left the room, her footsteps fading into the silence.

---

The next day, the workers whispered of Darshana's sudden disappearance. Some claimed he had fled, others that he had been taken by the spirits of the rock. Only the guards and a select few in the court knew the truth, and they kept it buried as deeply as Darshana's body.

But the whispers did not stop. If anything, they grew louder, mingling with tales of curses and omens. The rock seemed to exude an almost palpable malice, its presence looming over the camp like a living entity.

Kashyapa walked the grounds, his head held high, but inside he felt the cracks spreading. Every shadow seemed to harbor a threat, every glance a potential betrayal. He told himself that Sigiriya would be his legacy, a monument to his reign that would outlast time itself. Yet in his heart, he could not shake the fear that it was becoming something else entirely—a monument to his own descent.

The Lion Rock had claimed its second sacrifice. Kashyapa knew it would not be the last.

# CHAPTER 12: THE CURSE DEEPENS

The fortress of Sigiriya loomed larger with each passing day, its skeletal scaffolding reaching toward the heavens like an offering to the gods. Yet, an unnatural silence had fallen over the construction site. Workers moved hesitantly, their eyes darting to every shadow, their voices barely above whispers. The recent events—Darshana's sudden disappearance and the growing tales of curses—had taken their toll. Fear clung to the air like a miasma, choking the life from the camp.

In his chambers, Kashyapa sat across from Varuni. The mystic's dark eyes were unreadable, her expression calm despite the storm of rumors swirling through the court. Between them, a brazier burned low, its embers casting flickering shadows on the walls.

"The workers are afraid," Kashyapa said, his voice tight. "They speak of Darshana's ghost haunting the site, of curses and omens. How am I to drive them forward when they believe they are building their own tomb?"

Varuni leaned forward, her tone soothing but firm. "Fear is a powerful tool, Your Majesty. It can paralyze, yes, but it can also motivate. Darshana's death was a necessity, a sacrifice to the rock. The whispers of his ghost are nothing more than the imaginations of frightened men."

"And if they are not?" Kashyapa asked, his voice barely above a whisper. "What if the rock truly is cursed?"

Varuni's gaze hardened. "Sigiriya is not cursed," she said. "It is powerful. And power always comes with a cost. Embrace it, Your Majesty, and you will find that the fears of others are but noise against your destiny."

---

Despite Varuni's assurances, the whispers of Darshana's ghost persisted. Workers claimed to see his shadow moving across the scaffolding, hear his voice in the wind, and feel his presence in the chill of the night. One laborer swore he had seen Darshana's face in the reflection of the rock pool, his eyes burning with accusation. Another refused to climb the scaffolding after hearing footsteps above him when no one else was there.

The fear reached a boiling point when a worker fell to his death from the upper levels. Though it was deemed an accident, the others took it as a sign. Many refused to continue, and construction slowed to a crawl. Kashyapa's fury was palpable, his anger seeping into every corner of the camp. He summoned his foremen, his commanders, and Varuni to the great hall, his voice echoing off the stone walls.

"This fortress will be completed," he declared, his tone as unyielding as the rock itself. "I do not care for your ghosts or your curses. Sigiriya is my legacy, and I will not have it marred by cowardice. Any man who refuses to work will be dealt with as a traitor."

The room fell silent, the weight of his words pressing down on all who were present. The foremen exchanged uneasy glances, but none dared to speak. Only Varuni seemed unfazed, her gaze steady as she watched Kashyapa.

---

The following day, Kashyapa walked the site himself, his presence a stark reminder of his resolve. He moved among the workers, his eyes scanning their faces for any sign of defiance. Most avoided his gaze, their fear of him eclipsing their fear of the supposed curse. Yet, the unease lingered, a shadow that no decree could banish.

As he ascended the scaffolding, Kashyapa felt a strange pull toward the highest point of the construction. The view from the summit was breathtaking, the jungle stretching out like an emerald sea. But the serenity was short-lived. As he stood there, a gust of wind rushed past him, carrying with it a faint, chilling whisper.

"You cannot escape me."

Kashyapa froze, his heart pounding. He turned quickly, but there was no one there. The wind died down, and the whisper faded into silence. Shaking off the moment, he descended the scaffolding, his mind racing. Was it his guilt playing tricks on him, or something more?

In the days that followed, Kashyapa's paranoia deepened. He began to see Darshana's face in his dreams, his once-loyal architect's expression twisted with rage and sorrow. The visions grew more vivid, more insistent, until Kashyapa could no longer dismiss them as mere nightmares.

One night, he awoke in a cold sweat, his breathing ragged. The room was dark, but he could feel a presence, a weight in the air that pressed down on him like a physical force. He reached for the lamp beside his bed, but before he could light it, a voice echoed through the chamber.

"Why did you betray me?"

Kashyapa's blood ran cold. He turned toward the sound, but the room was empty. The voice came again, closer this time. "Why did you kill me?"

"Enough!" Kashyapa shouted, his voice trembling with both anger and fear. "You are dead, Darshana. You have no power here."

The voice fell silent, and the oppressive weight lifted. Kashyapa sat in the darkness, his hands gripping the edge of the bed, his mind a whirlwind of fear and defiance. If Darshana's ghost truly haunted Sigiriya, then it was a foe he would face like any other. He would not be cowed, not by the living or the dead.

The next morning, Kashyapa ordered a series of rituals to cleanse the site. Varuni oversaw the ceremonies, her chants echoing through the jungle as offerings were made to the spirits of the rock. The workers watched from a distance, their expressions a mix of hope and skepticism. For some, the rituals were a comfort; for others, they were little more than a hollow gesture.

Yet, despite the rituals, the whispers did not cease. The workers continued to speak of Darshana's ghost, of the rock's insatiable hunger for sacrifice. Kashyapa's decrees grew harsher, his punishments for disobedience more severe. The fear that had once united the camp now threatened to tear it apart.

Varuni remained a constant presence at Kashyapa's side, her calm demeanor a stark contrast to the chaos around her. "You are strong, Your Majesty," she said one evening as they stood on the terrace overlooking the site. "Stronger than the fears of lesser men. Sigiriya will be your greatest triumph, but only if you stay the course."

Kashyapa nodded, his resolve hardening once more. The rock would not break him. The whispers would not break him. He would see Sigiriya completed, no matter the cost.

But as he looked out over the fortress, he could not shake the feeling that it was no longer his creation. It had taken on a life of its own, a force that demanded more with each passing day. And Kashyapa knew, deep in his soul, that the cost would be higher than he could imagine.

# CHAPTER 13: THE FORTRESS RISES

T he sun rose over Sigiriya, casting a golden glow over the nearly completed fortress. The scaffolding that had once dominated the site was now sparse, replaced by gleaming walls and intricate designs. At the base of the rock, the water gardens shimmered, their reflective pools and flowing channels a marvel of engineering. Towering above it all, the lion's gate stood as a testament to Kashyapa's ambition, its carved paws gripping the stone with an air of majesty and defiance.

For all its grandeur, Sigiriya was no longer just a fortress or a palace. To Kashyapa, it was a throne—a divine seat that elevated him above mortal men. From here, he would rule not just with power but with the blessing of the gods. And yet, the whispers of fear and betrayal lingered, an undercurrent that threatened to drown his triumph.

As the day of the celebration approached, Kashyapa's court was abuzz with activity. Courtiers prepared elaborate ceremonies, musicians rehearsed their performances, and workers put the final touches on the frescoes that adorned the walls. The paintings depicted celestial maidens, their graceful forms floating amidst clouds, a vision of beauty and serenity that contrasted sharply with the unease that still hung over the site.

Varuni remained at Kashyapa's side, her calm presence a steadying force amidst the chaos. "The people will see this fortress for what it is," she said. "A symbol of your greatness, Your Majesty. They will bow before you, not out of fear, but out of reverence."

Kashyapa nodded, though his expression betrayed a flicker of doubt. "Let us hope they see it that way," he said. "Too many have whispered of curses and ghosts. This celebration must silence those whispers."

The day of the celebration dawned clear and bright. Delegates from across the kingdom arrived, their processions winding through the jungle to the base of Sigiriya. The atmosphere was festive, with banners fluttering in the breeze and the sounds of drums and flutes filling the air. The workers, who had labored tirelessly for months, were allowed a rare reprieve, their faces lighting up as they took in the fruits of their efforts.

Kashyapa stood on the terrace overlooking the gathering, his robes of gold and crimson catching the sunlight. He raised his arms, and the crowd fell silent.

"Behold Sigiriya," he declared, his voice carrying across the assembly. "This is not merely a fortress. It is a testament to our strength, our ingenuity, and our faith. From this throne, we shall rise above all who would challenge us. Let this day mark the beginning of a new era, one of glory and prosperity for our kingdom."

The crowd erupted into applause, their cheers echoing off the rock. Kashyapa allowed himself a moment of pride, the weight of his doubts lifting as he basked in their adulation.

As the celebration continued, guests mingled in the gardens, marveling at the intricate water channels and the towering frescoes. Musicians played lively tunes, and dancers performed beneath the shadow of the lion's gate. For a time, it seemed as though the unease that had plagued Sigiriya was but a distant memory.

But the peace was short-lived.

Amidst the revelry, a scream pierced the air. The music stopped abruptly, and the crowd turned toward the source of the sound. Near the edge of one of the pools, a man lay motionless, his body contorted in a way that was unnatural and horrifying. Those closest to him recoiled, their faces pale with fear.

Kashyapa descended the terrace with swift strides, his guards clearing a path through the crowd. He knelt beside the body, his stomach twisting as he took in the sight. The man's eyes were wide open, his expression frozen in terror. There were no visible wounds, yet his lifelessness was unmistakable.

"What happened?" Kashyapa demanded, his voice sharp.

A servant stepped forward hesitantly, her hands trembling. "I-I do not know, Your Majesty," she stammered. "One moment he was laughing, and the next..." She trailed off, her gaze fixed on the body.

Varuni appeared at Kashyapa's side, her expression grim. She placed a hand on his shoulder, leaning close to speak in a low voice. "The rock claims what it wills," she said. "This death is a warning. There are those who still defy your reign, and the rock's anger will not be sated until they are dealt with."

Kashyapa's jaw tightened. He rose to his feet, addressing the crowd. "This man's death is a tragedy, but it will not overshadow this day," he said. "Let his passing remind us of the cost of greatness. Sigiriya demands much of us, but we shall endure."

The crowd murmured their agreement, though their unease was palpable. The celebration continued, but the mood had shifted. The music was subdued, the laughter forced. Kashyapa could feel the tension building once more, like a storm gathering on the horizon.

That night, as the guests departed and the workers returned to their quarters, Kashyapa remained on the terrace, staring out over the fortress. The events of the day weighed heavily on him, the man's lifeless face etched into his memory.

"Another death," he muttered to himself. "How many more will Sigiriya take?"

Varuni stepped out of the shadows, her voice calm and measured. "The rock tests your resolve, Your Majesty. Each death strengthens its foundation, binds it to your will."

Kashyapa turned to her, his eyes weary. "And what of my will? How much must I sacrifice before Sigiriya is truly mine?"

Varuni's gaze was steady. "Greatness demands sacrifice. You have always known this. But take heart, Your Majesty. The fortress rises, and with it, your legacy."

Kashyapa nodded slowly, her words offering little comfort. As he gazed upon Sigiriya, its walls bathed in moonlight, he could not shake the feeling that the fortress was no longer his creation. It had become something else entirely, something that demanded more than he could ever give. And yet, he could not stop. Sigiriya must be completed, no matter the cost.

# CHAPTER 14: A KINGDOM IN FEAR

The skies above Sigiriya darkened, though no storm clouds had gathered. The atmosphere was heavy, charged with an unnatural energy that seemed to seep into the very stones of the fortress. Flocks of crows circled the rock, their harsh cries echoing across the jungle. The workers, already uneasy after the celebration's tragic end, moved about their tasks with quick, furtive glances at the sky. It was as if the land itself was warning them of something yet to come.

Kashyapa stood on the upper terrace, watching the crows with a furrowed brow. Behind him, Varuni approached silently, her presence as unsettling as ever.

"The omens grow stronger," she said, her voice low but firm. "The rock stirs, Your Majesty. It senses the unrest within your court."

Kashyapa's jaw tightened. "Let it stir," he replied. "I will not falter. Sigiriya will stand, and with it, my reign."

Varuni tilted her head, her dark eyes fixed on him. "Your resolve is admirable," she said. "But resolve alone cannot silence the whispers of rebellion. The nobles grow restless, and their discontent feeds the chaos that surrounds us."

Kashyapa turned to face her, his expression hard. "Then I will root out the dissenters myself. Let them plot in shadows. I will bring them into the light and make an example of them."

---

The omens were not confined to Sigiriya. Across the kingdom, reports of strange phenomena began to spread. Villagers spoke of rain tinged red as blood, its droplets staining the earth. Small tremors shook the land, unsettling both the people and their livestock. In one remote village, a temple's sacred statue cracked down the center without warning, an event many took as a sign of divine displeasure.

These occurrences only fueled the growing unease within Kashyapa's court. The nobles gathered in secret, their conversations laced with fear and suspicion.

"The gods are punishing us," one whispered, his voice trembling. "Kashyapa has angered them with his hubris."

"It is not the gods we should fear," another countered. "It is the king himself. His paranoia grows with each passing day. How long before he turns his wrath upon us?"

---

Kashyapa's suspicions had indeed deepened. He called private meetings with his guards, issuing orders to monitor the nobles more closely. Letters were intercepted, conversations overheard, and alliances scrutinized. The king's spies reported whispers of rebellion, though no concrete plans had yet emerged.

Commander Vihara approached Kashyapa one evening, his demeanor cautious. "Your Majesty," he began, "I must speak plainly. The unrest within the court grows stronger. The nobles question your decisions, your... methods."

Kashyapa's gaze sharpened. "My methods are necessary to secure this kingdom. Do they think Moggallana will show them mercy if he returns? Weakness will destroy us faster than any rebellion."

"Even so," Vihara said carefully, "if the court turns against you, we may face an enemy from within as well as without."

Kashyapa's lips thinned into a hard line. "Then I will crush them both. Prepare the army, Commander. Let the nobles see that rebellion will not be tolerated."

---

The days that followed were marked by a tense stillness, as if the kingdom itself held its breath. Kashyapa's display of military strength sent a clear message, but it did little to quell the whispers. The court's loyalty was fractured, and the omens continued to feed their fears.

One night, Kashyapa was awoken by a loud crack that reverberated through the fortress. He rushed to the terrace, where Varuni was already waiting. Below, the workers had gathered near the lion's gate, their torches casting eerie shadows on the rock. Kashyapa descended quickly, his heart pounding.

At the base of the lion's gate, a massive fissure had appeared in one of the rock's carved paws. The workers murmured among themselves, their voices tinged with fear.

"The rock is angry," one said. "It demands more sacrifices."

Kashyapa silenced them with a raised hand. "Enough," he said, his voice firm. "This is no curse. It is merely a flaw in the stone, nothing more."

The workers fell silent, though their expressions betrayed their disbelief. Kashyapa turned to Varuni, who stood at his side, her gaze fixed on the fissure.

"What does this mean?" Kashyapa asked, his voice low.

Varuni's expression was unreadable. "The rock tests you again," she said. "It demands unwavering faith. Do not let their fear infect you, Your Majesty. Show them that you are stronger than any omen."

Kashyapa nodded, though the unease in his chest remained.

---

In the days that followed, Kashyapa ordered the fissure repaired, the workers toiling under his watchful eye. But the damage had already been done. The fissure became a symbol, a physical manifestation of the fears that had taken root in the hearts of the court and the workers alike.

The whispers of rebellion grew louder, their reach extending beyond the palace walls. Kashyapa's spies reported secret meetings in the homes of nobles, alliances forged in the shadows. And amidst it all, the omens continued: the crows, the red rain, the tremors.

Kashyapa stood on the terrace one evening, staring out at the jungle as the sun dipped below the horizon. Varuni joined him, her presence as enigmatic as ever.

"The court conspires against me," Kashyapa said, his voice heavy. "They would see me fall before Sigiriya is even complete."

Varuni placed a hand on his shoulder, her touch cool and grounding. "You are the king," she said. "Their whispers are meaningless. Sigiriya will be your shield, your strength. But you must act decisively. Show them that you will not be swayed."

Kashyapa turned to her, his gaze searching. "And if they rebel?"

Varuni's eyes gleamed in the fading light. "Then you crush them. Let their blood feed the rock. Only then will Sigiriya truly be yours."

As the first stars appeared in the night sky, Kashyapa made his decision. The time for hesitation was over. If rebellion was brewing, he would extinguish it before it could take hold. The kingdom was his, and he would not let it slip away.

# CHAPTER 15: VARUNI'S PROPHECY

The winds howled around Sigiriya, carrying with them the whispers of the jungle below. Kashyapa stood on the Lion Terrace, staring into the horizon where the sun dipped behind the dense foliage. The fortress, his divine seat, seemed almost alive under the twilight, its golden frescoes reflecting a fiery glow. But for all its beauty, Kashyapa felt unease gnawing at the edges of his mind, an insistent reminder of a future he could not escape.

Varuni approached silently, her footsteps soft against the stone. She carried an air of solemnity that sent a chill down Kashyapa's spine.

"You summoned me, Your Majesty?" she asked, her voice as calm as the still pools in the gardens below.

Kashyapa turned to her, his eyes shadowed with exhaustion and fear. "The omens have not ceased," he said. "The tremors, the whispers, the cursed rains. Tell me, Varuni. What do they mean?"

Varuni's gaze was piercing as she stepped closer. "They are warnings," she said. "The rock speaks of a reckoning, of a fate that draws near. Your brother, Moggallana, gathers strength in exile. He will return, and when he does, he will bring with him the storm that will test your reign."

Kashyapa's jaw tightened. "Moggallana?" he repeated, the name like a curse on his tongue. "He is no threat to me. This fortress is impenetrable. My army is loyal."

Varuni shook her head. "Fate does not bend to walls or swords," she said. "I have seen it, Your Majesty. You will face Moggallana on the battlefield, and there..." She hesitated, her voice faltering for the first time.

"And there what?" Kashyapa demanded, stepping closer, his tone edged with desperation.

Varuni's expression softened, though her words cut like a blade. "And there, you will fall."

---

The words hung in the air, a grim prophecy that settled deep into Kashyapa's chest. He turned away from her, his hands clenching into fists. "No," he said, his voice firm. "I will not die by his hand. I will not let fate dictate my end."

Varuni watched him carefully. "Fate can be defied," she said. "But only if you act with foresight and strength. Every decision you make from this moment onward must be precise, calculated. Seek my guidance, and together, we may yet shape a different outcome."

Kashyapa nodded, his resolve hardening. "Then guide me, Varuni. Show me the path that leads to victory."

---

In the days that followed, Kashyapa became consumed by Varuni's prophecy. He consulted her at every turn, seeking insight into his dreams, his fears, and the movements of his court. Varuni's cryptic advice, though maddening at times, seemed to hold a strange clarity when the pieces fell into place.

"The army must be strengthened," she said during one meeting. "Not just in numbers, but in loyalty. Reward those who have stood by you and root out those whose loyalty wavers."

Kashyapa followed her counsel, bestowing titles and lands upon his most trusted commanders while quietly removing those who had shown signs of dissent. The army's morale improved, though the court's unrest persisted.

"And the people?" Kashyapa asked during another consultation. "What of their faith in me?"

Varuni's expression grew thoughtful. "The people must see you not as a man, but as a god-king," she said. "Sigiriya is your throne, but it is also your altar. Perform rituals, invoke the favor of the gods, and let the people witness your divine right to rule."

Kashyapa took her advice to heart, organizing grand ceremonies atop Sigiriya. Offerings were made, chants filled the air, and the people were invited to witness their king's communion with the gods. For a time, the fear that had gripped the kingdom seemed to ease, replaced by awe and reverence.

---

Yet, despite these efforts, Kashyapa's own fears did not abate. The vision of his death on the battlefield haunted him, creeping into his dreams and waking thoughts. He saw himself surrounded by enemies, the clang of swords and the cries of war echoing in his ears. He saw Moggallana's face, twisted with triumph, as the final blow was struck.

One night, he confronted Varuni in her quarters, his desperation laid bare.

"You told me I could defy fate," he said, his voice trembling. "But every step I take seems to lead me closer to it. What more can I do?"

Varuni regarded him with a mixture of pity and resolve. "Fate is a river, Your Majesty," she said. "It flows toward its end, but the current can be diverted. You must find the source of your fear and confront it head-on. Only then can you hope to change its course."

Kashyapa's brow furrowed. "The source of my fear?"

"Moggallana," Varuni said simply. "He is the shadow that haunts you. You must draw him out, face him not as a brother, but as a rival. Only by defeating him can you break the chains of this prophecy."

Determined to take control of his fate, Kashyapa began preparations for war. Scouts were sent to gather intelligence on Moggallana's movements, while the army was drilled relentlessly. Kashyapa himself trained alongside his soldiers, honing his skills with a single-minded intensity.

Varuni continued to guide him, her advice both practical and enigmatic. "The battlefield is not just a place of strength," she said. "It is a place of strategy, of deception. Use the rock to your advantage. Make Sigiriya a fortress they cannot breach."

Kashyapa took her words to heart, ordering the construction of additional defenses and hidden pathways within the fortress. Every aspect of Sigiriya was scrutinized, its strengths fortified and its weaknesses addressed.

As the preparations continued, the tension within the kingdom grew. The omens persisted, their warnings becoming more dire. One morning, the jungle around Sigiriya was found littered with the bodies of dead birds, their feathers blackened as if scorched by fire. The people whispered of divine punishment, their faith in Kashyapa wavering once more.

Kashyapa stood on the terrace, staring out at the eerie sight. Varuni joined him, her presence a steadying force.

"The signs grow darker," Kashyapa said, his voice heavy. "Is this the gods' way of telling me I cannot escape my fate?"

Varuni placed a hand on his shoulder. "The gods test you," she said. "But they have not abandoned you. Show them your strength, Your Majesty. Prove that you are worthy of the throne you have built."

Kashyapa nodded, his resolve hardening. The path ahead was fraught with danger, but he would not falter. He would face Moggallana, and he would defy the prophecy that sought to claim him.

As the sun set over Sigiriya, casting the fortress in a blood-red light, Kashyapa vowed to himself that he would rise above the shadows of fate. The battle was coming, and he would meet it with the full force of his will. For Sigiriya. For his legacy. For his survival.

# CHAPTER 16: VIHARA'S LOYALTY TESTED

The crackle of torches illuminated the barracks as Commander Vihara paced back and forth. The air was thick with tension, an unspoken unrest rippling through the ranks of Kashyapa's army. Soldiers murmured in hushed tones, their faces etched with doubt. The recent omens and the king's escalating paranoia had seeped into their spirits like poison. Vihara could feel it—a fragile balance on the verge of collapse.

"Order," Vihara barked, his voice slicing through the murmurs. "You will maintain discipline. The king demands it, and so do I."

The soldiers straightened, but their eyes betrayed them. Fear. Doubt. Disillusionment. Vihara clenched his fists. He had fought alongside many of these men for years, and now, one by one, he saw them faltering.

After the assembly dispersed, Vihara retreated to his quarters, his mind heavy with worry. The whispers had reached him, too. Rumors of rebellion, of nobles conspiring with Moggallana, and of Kashyapa's grip on reality slipping away. Vihara's loyalty had never wavered before, but now... now, he wasn't sure what to believe.

---

Kashyapa summoned Vihara the next morning. The king's chambers were dimly lit, the curtains drawn against the harsh sunlight. A brazier burned low, casting flickering shadows on the walls. Kashyapa sat at a carved stone table, his fingers drumming against its surface. His eyes, sunken from sleepless nights, bore into Vihara as he entered.

"Commander," Kashyapa said, his voice cold and clipped. "Reports have reached me that discipline in the ranks is failing. Soldiers questioning their orders, loyalty wavering. Is this true?"

Vihara hesitated, choosing his words carefully. "There is unrest, Your Majesty," he admitted. "But it is not rebellion. The men are... uneasy. The omens, the whispers. They have sown doubt."

Kashyapa's hand slammed against the table, the sound echoing through the chamber. "Doubt?" he snarled. "Doubt leads to betrayal, and betrayal leads to ruin. I will not have my army crumble because of cowards and fools."

"Your Majesty," Vihara said, his tone measured, "the men need reassurance. They need to see strength, not suspicion. If you demand loyalty, you must also inspire it."

Kashyapa's eyes narrowed. "Are you questioning me, Commander?"

Vihara stiffened. "Never, Your Majesty. My loyalty is to you and the crown. But I must speak the truth if we are to hold this army together."

---

Despite Vihara's careful words, Kashyapa's paranoia latched onto the conversation like a leech. That evening, he called Varuni to his chambers, his mind racing with suspicions.

"Vihara," Kashyapa began, his voice low, "he says he is loyal, but his words... they reek of doubt. Can I trust him?"

Varuni's gaze was steady, her expression unreadable. "Trust is a fragile thing, Your Majesty," she said. "But Vihara has served you faithfully for years. If his loyalty wavers now, it is not out of malice, but fear. Strengthen his resolve, and he will remain by your side."

Kashyapa frowned. "And if he does not?"

Varuni's lips curved into a faint smile. "Then you know what must be done."

---

The next day, Kashyapa called a gathering of his commanders and soldiers in the main courtyard of Sigiriya. The sun blazed overhead, casting long shadows across the assembled ranks. Kashyapa stood atop the stone steps, his presence imposing as he addressed the crowd.

"My warriors," he began, his voice carrying across the courtyard. "You have sworn your loyalty to me, to this kingdom, and to Sigiriya. But loyalty is meaningless without action. I have heard whispers of doubt among you, whispers that threaten to weaken us from within."

He paused, his gaze sweeping over the crowd. "Let me be clear. There is no room for weakness in this army. The omens you fear are nothing compared to the wrath I will unleash upon those who betray me. Stand with me, and you will share in the glory of my reign. Stand against me, and you will fall."

The soldiers exchanged uneasy glances, but many nodded, their resolve seemingly bolstered by the king's words. Vihara stood among them, his face expressionless as he listened. He could feel Kashyapa's eyes on him, probing, testing.

---

Later that evening, Vihara was summoned to Kashyapa's private chambers once more. The atmosphere was tense, the air thick with unspoken accusations.

"Commander," Kashyapa said, his tone sharp. "Do you stand with me, or against me?"

Vihara met the king's gaze, his voice steady. "I have always stood with you, Your Majesty. And I always will."

Kashyapa leaned back in his chair, studying him. "Good," he said finally. "Because if I find even a hint of treachery among my commanders, there will be no mercy."

Vihara nodded, but as he left the chamber, he could not shake the feeling that his loyalty alone would not be enough to satisfy the king's growing paranoia.

In the days that followed, the tension within the army began to ease. Vihara's efforts to maintain order and discipline bore fruit, and Kashyapa's fiery speech seemed to have reignited the soldiers' resolve. But beneath the surface, cracks remained. The omens persisted, and the whispers of rebellion grew quieter, but not because they had ceased. They had merely gone deeper underground, hidden from the king's spies.

Kashyapa, for his part, threw himself into the completion of Sigiriya. The fortress was his shield, his weapon, and his legacy. He could feel the tide turning, the storm brewing on the horizon. Moggallana's return was inevitable, but Kashyapa was determined to meet him on the battlefield, his army and his fortress unyielding.

Yet, even as he prepared for war, a question lingered in his mind. Could he truly trust those closest to him? Or was the greatest threat to his reign not his brother, but the cracks within his own walls?

# CHAPTER 17:
# AHALYA'S SECRET

The library of Sigiriya was a sanctuary of knowledge and secrets, its walls lined with scrolls and tablets chronicling centuries of history. Ahalya moved through its shadowed aisles, her fingers brushing against the parchments as though the answers she sought might reveal themselves through touch alone. She had always prided herself on being a chronicler, a silent observer of the court's intrigue. But the parchment in her hands now felt heavier than any she had held before. The truth it contained had the power to unravel the kingdom.

The evidence was clear: records of clandestine meetings between certain nobles and Moggallana's allies. More damning still were fragments of correspondence implicating these nobles in King Dhatusena's death. Ahalya's heart raced as she pieced the timeline together. Dhatusena's murder had not been solely Kashyapa's doing. It had been orchestrated, the strings pulled by those who now surrounded Kashyapa's throne.

The revelation left Ahalya shaken. She sat at a stone desk, the parchment spread before her, the flickering lamplight casting shifting shadows over the damning words. Her mind raced with possibilities. Should she bring this to Kashyapa? He was already consumed by paranoia, his trust in those around him tenuous at best. This revelation could push him over the edge, driving him to purge his court and plunge the kingdom into chaos.

But to withhold it was no less perilous. Moggallana's forces were gathering strength, emboldened by the divisions within Sigiriya. If these conspirators remained in the king's inner circle, they could sabotage Kashyapa from within when the final confrontation came.

Ahalya's thoughts were interrupted by a faint creak. She froze, her breath catching. The library was meant to be deserted at this hour. Footsteps echoed softly against the stone floor, drawing closer. She quickly rolled the parchment and tucked it into the folds of her robe, extinguishing the lamp as she pressed herself into the shadows.

A figure emerged, silhouetted against the faint light filtering through the arched windows. It was one of the palace guards, his eyes scanning the room. Ahalya held her breath, her pulse thundering in her ears. After a moment, the guard turned and left, his footsteps fading into silence.

Ahalya exhaled slowly, her fingers trembling as she adjusted her robes. She knew she couldn't stay here. The parchment was too dangerous to leave behind, and her presence would raise questions if discovered. Clutching the scroll tightly, she slipped out of the library, her steps light and deliberate as she made her way back to her chambers.

---

The next morning, Ahalya sat by her window, staring out at the sprawling gardens below. The fortress buzzed with activity, oblivious to the storm brewing within its walls. She turned the parchment over in her hands, her thoughts a tangled web of fear and duty.

Varuni's voice echoed in her mind, unbidden. The mystic had often spoken of balance, of the delicate threads that held the kingdom together. Ahalya had never trusted Varuni fully, but her words now carried a haunting resonance. This truth could shatter that balance, tipping Sigiriya into ruin.

But could she bear the burden of silence? Could she watch the kingdom crumble, knowing she had the means to prevent it?

---

Ahalya sought out Commander Vihara. Of all those in Kashyapa's inner circle, he was the one she trusted most. His loyalty to the king was unwavering, but he also possessed a pragmatism that set him apart from the sycophants and schemers of the court.

She found him in the training yard, overseeing drills. The clang of swords and the shouts of soldiers filled the air, a stark contrast to the quiet turmoil within her. Vihara noticed her approach and dismissed the soldiers, his expression curious but guarded.

"Ahalya," he said, his tone neutral. "To what do I owe this visit?"

She hesitated, glancing around to ensure they were alone. "Commander, I need to speak with you. In private."

Vihara's brows knit together, but he nodded, leading her to a secluded alcove. "What is it?" he asked.

Ahalya produced the parchment, her hands trembling slightly as she handed it to him. "Read this," she said. "And tell me what you would do."

Vihara unrolled the scroll, his eyes scanning the text. As he read, his expression darkened, his jaw tightening. When he finished, he looked up at her, his gaze sharp.

"Where did you find this?" he demanded.

"In the library," Ahalya replied. "Buried among old records. I don't know who else has seen it, but if this information is true…"

"It changes everything," Vihara finished, his voice grim. "These nobles… they've been playing a dangerous game. If the king finds out…"

"That's what I fear," Ahalya said. "Kashyapa's paranoia is already consuming him. If he learns of this, he might see enemies everywhere. It could destroy what's left of his court."

Vihara nodded slowly. "But if we do nothing, these conspirators will undermine him when we can least afford it. Moggallana's return is inevitable. The kingdom cannot face him divided."

---

The two of them deliberated late into the night, weighing their options. By the time they parted, a fragile plan had taken shape. Ahalya would continue to investigate, gathering more evidence to ensure the truth could not be denied. Vihara, meanwhile, would keep a closer watch on the nobles, subtly testing their loyalties without raising suspicion.

But as Ahalya returned to her chambers, the weight of the parchment pressed heavily against her chest. She had chosen to act, but the path ahead was fraught with danger. One misstep, and the kingdom she sought to save could be plunged into chaos.

As she lay awake that night, the fortress around her silent and still, Ahalya couldn't shake the feeling that the walls of Sigiriya were closing in. The truth she carried was a burden, but it was also a weapon. And she knew all too well that weapons, once drawn, could not easily be sheathed.

# CHAPTER 18: THE SACRED POOL

The golden light of dawn bathed Sigiriya, but to Kashyapa, the beauty of the morning did little to ease the storm within. Each step he took along the winding paths of the fortress felt heavier, burdened by the weight of prophecies, conspiracies, and his own haunting visions. Today, Varuni had summoned him to a secluded part of the fortress, a place she claimed held the key to unraveling his fate.

She led him through a hidden passage, her movements deliberate and confident. The air grew cooler as they descended, the stone walls narrowing around them. Kashyapa's footsteps echoed, each sound amplified in the eerie silence. Finally, the passage opened into a cavern, illuminated by shafts of light filtering through cracks in the rock above. At its center was a pool, its surface so still it mirrored the jagged ceiling perfectly.

"This is the sacred pool of visions," Varuni said, her voice reverent. "The ancients believed that it could show glimpses of the future to those strong enough to face the truth."

Kashyapa's eyes narrowed as he approached the water. "You believe this will show me my fate?"

Varuni stepped beside him, her expression enigmatic. "The water reveals possibilities, not certainties. What you see will depend on your own soul, your fears, and your desires."

For a moment, Kashyapa hesitated. But the pull of the unknown, the chance to understand what lay ahead, was too strong to resist. He knelt by the pool, the cold stone biting into his knees as he leaned forward. The surface of the water shimmered, rippling as if sensing his presence. Then, it stilled, and Kashyapa's reflection began to change.

At first, he saw himself as he wished to be: standing triumphant on the Lion Terrace, his people bowing before him, Sigiriya gleaming like a beacon of divine power. But the vision shifted, the edges darkening. The cheers of the crowd turned to cries of fear as the sky above grew thick with smoke.

Kashyapa saw a battlefield, chaotic and blood-soaked. His army, once disciplined and unyielding, was in disarray, retreating under the relentless charge of enemy forces. An elephant—his own mount—turned and fled, its panic mirroring the despair in Kashyapa's heart. And there, in the center of the carnage, he saw himself. His armor was dented and bloodied, his face twisted with anguish. A sword plunged into his chest, and he fell, the light fading from his eyes as the vision dissolved into darkness.

Kashyapa gasped, pulling back from the pool. His heart raced, and his hands trembled as he pressed them against the cold stone floor. "This cannot be," he muttered, his voice trembling. "It will not be."

Varuni knelt beside him, her tone measured. "The pool shows one path, Your Majesty. But every path can be altered. You have the power to change what you have seen, but only if you act with wisdom and resolve."

Kashyapa's gaze hardened as he rose to his feet. "Then I will change it. I will defy the vision, just as I will defy those who seek to overthrow me."

The vision from the pool consumed Kashyapa's thoughts as he

returned to the surface. He summoned his commanders, his advisors, and even the artisans working on Sigiriya. His orders were precise and unyielding. The fortress's defenses were to be strengthened, its hidden pathways fortified, and its resources stockpiled for a siege.

"Leave nothing to chance," Kashyapa commanded, his voice cutting through the room. "When Moggallana comes, we will be ready. Sigiriya will not fall, and neither will I."

Commander Vihara exchanged a glance with Ahalya, who stood at the edge of the chamber, her expression unreadable. Both could sense the urgency—and the desperation—in Kashyapa's tone. The king was no longer preparing for war; he was waging one against fate itself.

---

As the fortress buzzed with activity, Kashyapa returned to Varuni, seeking her counsel again and again. "Tell me how to defeat him," he demanded one evening, his frustration boiling over. "You said I could alter the vision. How?"

Varuni regarded him with a calm that only infuriated him further. "Victory is not achieved through strength alone," she said. "It requires cunning, sacrifice, and an unshakable will. You must outthink Moggallana, anticipate his every move. And above all, you must not let fear cloud your judgment."

Kashyapa's fists clenched at his sides. "Fear?" he spat. "I am not afraid. I will face him, and I will win."

Varuni's lips curved into a faint smile. "Then you are already stronger than the vision. But strength must be tempered with wisdom, or it will destroy you."

---

Despite Varuni's reassurances, Kashyapa could not shake the shadow of the vision. He began to see signs of its fulfillment everywhere. A horse stumbled and fell during a training drill, its rider thrown violently to the ground. A tree struck by lightning split in two, its charred remains resembling the battlefield he had seen. Even the wind seemed to whisper of doom as it howled through the fortress.

Each omen drove him to push harder, to prepare more obsessively. His commanders grew weary under the weight of his demands, but none dared voice their concerns. Kashyapa's paranoia was palpable, an unspoken force that dominated every corner of Sigiriya.

One evening, as the sun dipped below the horizon, Ahalya approached Kashyapa in the great hall. She hesitated at the threshold, watching as he stared into the flames of the brazier, his face illuminated by its flickering light.

"Your Majesty," she said softly, stepping forward. "May I speak with you?"

Kashyapa turned, his expression hard but not unkind. "What is it, Ahalya?"

She hesitated, choosing her words carefully. "The men are loyal, but they grow weary. They fear not only Moggallana, but the strain this war places on them. Perhaps... perhaps it is time to remind them of your vision, of your strength. Inspire them, and they will follow you without question."

Kashyapa studied her for a moment, then nodded. "You are right," he said. "I will address them tomorrow. They must see that I am not a man bound by prophecy, but one who shapes his own destiny."

The next day, Kashyapa stood before his army on the Lion Terrace, the fortress sprawling behind him. His voice rang out, strong and unyielding.

"My warriors," he declared, "the visions of seers and the whispers of the fearful mean nothing before the will of a king. Sigiriya is our strength, our shield, and our sword. Together, we will stand against any who dare challenge us. Fate is not our master. We are the masters of our own destiny."

The soldiers cheered, their voices rising like a wave. For a moment, Kashyapa felt the weight of the vision lift. But as he gazed out over the assembled ranks, a flicker of doubt remained. The pool had shown him one possible future, and no matter how hard he tried, he could not banish the image of his own death.

As the cheers faded and the soldiers returned to their duties, Kashyapa stood alone on the terrace, staring into the horizon. The battle was coming, and with it, the test of his strength, his will, and his ability to defy the fate that sought to claim him.

# CHAPTER 19: THE CURSE CONSUMES

The oppressive heat of midday hung over Sigiriya, the air thick and unmoving. Despite the brilliant sunlight, shadows seemed to cling to the edges of the fortress, refusing to yield to the light. Kashyapa stood on the Lion Terrace, watching the dwindling lines of workers toiling below. The sound of chisels and hammers, once a constant rhythm of progress, had grown sporadic. Whispers of fear now filled the air where the crack of stone once reigned.

"Another group deserted last night," Commander Vihara reported, his voice heavy with resignation. "Three stonecutters, two masons, and an entire crew from the southern gardens."

Kashyapa's jaw clenched. "Cowards," he spat. "They abandon their duty at the first sign of hardship. They've allowed themselves to be consumed by superstition."

Vihara hesitated before responding. "The... occurrences have frightened them, Your Majesty. The whispers of voices in the tunnels, the apparitions some claim to have seen. And the deaths..."

Kashyapa turned sharply to face him, his eyes blazing. "The deaths were accidents," he said, his voice rising. "Weak minds see shadows and turn them into monsters. I will not have my fortress—my legacy—halted by their foolishness."

The stories of the workers had grown darker with each passing day. One claimed to have seen a pale figure standing at the edge of the scaffolding, only for it to vanish when approached. Another swore he heard faint whispers emanating from the unfinished tunnels, voices calling his name. Most unsettling were the deaths: a worker crushed under a mysteriously loosened stone, another found drowned in a shallow pool despite knowing how to swim. The workers whispered that Sigiriya itself was rebelling against its creator.

Varuni's presence only added to the unease. She moved through the site like a wraith, her calm demeanor contrasting sharply with the panic around her. To Kashyapa, she was a pillar of strength, her assurances soothing his fraying nerves. But to the workers, she was a harbinger, her cryptic words and unsettling gaze feeding their fears.

"The rock hungers," she said one evening as she stood with Kashyapa overlooking the site. "It demands sacrifices for the glory you seek to build."

Kashyapa's brows furrowed. "I've given it sacrifices," he said, his voice tinged with frustration. "Offerings, rituals... even Darshana."

Varuni's expression remained inscrutable. "Perhaps it is not the rock that must change," she said, "but the will of those who serve it. Strength must be forged in fear, or it will crumble under the weight of doubt."

Determined to restore order, Kashyapa summoned the remaining workers to the main courtyard. The men gathered reluctantly, their faces a mix of fear and defiance. Kashyapa stood before them, his presence commanding.

"I have heard the whispers," he began, his voice echoing off the stone walls. "I know your fears. But let me tell you this: fear is the tool of the weak. Sigiriya is not cursed. It is a testament to our strength, our unity, and our devotion to a greater purpose. Those who abandon it betray not only me but themselves."

He paused, his gaze sweeping over the crowd. "From this day forward, desertion will be met with the harshest punishment. The work will continue, and we will succeed. You will not falter. Not while I stand among you."

The crowd murmured uneasily, but none dared speak. Kashyapa motioned to Vihara, who stepped forward with a group of guards. "Bring out the deserters," Kashyapa commanded.

One by one, the captured workers were dragged into the courtyard. Their faces were pale, their bodies trembling. Kashyapa's voice was cold as he addressed them.

"You were given the honor of building a legacy," he said. "And you threw it away for the sake of your cowardice. Such betrayal cannot be tolerated."

He raised his hand, signaling the guards. The punishment was swift and brutal, carried out before the eyes of the assembled workers. The message was clear: loyalty was not optional. By the time the executions were over, a heavy silence had fallen over the courtyard.

---

That night, Kashyapa sat alone in his chambers, staring into the flickering flames of the brazier. The faces of the deserters haunted him, their fear and desperation etched into his mind. He told himself it had been necessary, that their punishment would ensure the survival of the project. But a small, nagging voice whispered otherwise.

Varuni entered, her steps soft. She took a seat across from him, her dark eyes watching him intently. "You did what was required," she said, as if reading his thoughts.

Kashyapa's gaze remained fixed on the fire. "Did I?" he murmured. "Or have I become the very tyrant I sought to escape?"

Varuni's voice was gentle but firm. "Greatness demands sacrifice, Your Majesty. Weakness is a poison that spreads if left unchecked. You cannot build a legacy without hard choices."

Kashyapa looked at her, searching for reassurance in her enigmatic expression. "And what of the whispers? The apparitions? Are they weakness as well?"

Varuni leaned closer, her voice dropping to a whisper. "The rock remembers," she said. "Its power is older than any of us. But it has chosen you, Kashyapa. Do not let doubt steal what it has granted."

The following days saw a grim resurgence in activity. The workers, cowed by the executions, resumed their tasks with a desperate fervor. But the fear lingered, a shadow over every hammer stroke and chisel cut. The whispers in the tunnels grew louder, the apparitions more frequent. Even Kashyapa began to hear the voices, faint but unmistakable, calling his name in the dead of night.

One evening, as he walked alone along the terraces, he saw a figure standing at the edge of the cliff. It was a man, his silhouette stark against the moonlit sky. Kashyapa's heart raced as he approached, his hand instinctively reaching for the dagger at his side.

"Who are you?" he demanded.

The figure turned slowly, and Kashyapa's breath caught. It was Rajith, his face pale and his eyes hollow. "You cannot escape it," the apparition said, its voice echoing unnaturally. "The blood on your hands will drown you."

Kashyapa stumbled back, his pulse pounding in his ears. When he blinked, the figure was gone, leaving only the whispering wind in its wake.

The next morning, Kashyapa called for Varuni, his voice edged with urgency. "The visions grow stronger," he said. "Even I have seen them now. Tell me, Varuni. What must I do to silence them?"

Varuni's expression was unreadable as she replied. "The rock has its own will, Your Majesty. To appease it, you must prove your worth. Show it that you are unshakable, that your resolve is greater than any fear."

Kashyapa nodded, his resolve hardening once more. He would not falter. Sigiriya would stand, and his name would echo through eternity. But as he prepared to face the challenges ahead, a single thought lingered in his mind, as persistent as the whispers in the night:

Had he already lost himself to the curse he sought to defy?

# CHAPTER 20:
# THE RETURN OF
# MOGGALLANA

The morning air was thick with an unsettling calm, a silence that seemed to stretch over Sigiriya like a veil. Kashyapa stood on the western rampart, his gaze fixed on the jungle beyond. The once-lush greenery now felt like an enemy's shroud, concealing the threat that loomed just beyond his sight.

Commander Vihara approached swiftly, his armor catching the first rays of the sun. His expression was grim.

"Your Majesty," he said, bowing low. "The scouts have returned. Moggallana's army has crossed the Mahaweli River. They march with purpose, and their numbers are... considerable."

Kashyapa's jaw tightened. "How many?" he demanded.

"Thousands," Vihara replied. "Well-trained and heavily armed. They've brought war elephants, siege equipment. This is no raid, Your Majesty. This is an invasion."

For a moment, Kashyapa said nothing, his hands gripping the stone parapet. He felt the weight of his crown pressing heavier than ever, a burden that seemed to grow with each passing moment. But he could not afford hesitation. Not now.

"Sigiriya will stand," he said finally, his voice resolute. "Let them come. This fortress is a symbol of our strength, our unity. We will meet them with fire and steel."

---

The news spread quickly through the fortress. The courtyards buzzed with activity as soldiers prepared for the inevitable. Archers tested their bows, swordsmen sharpened their blades, and laborers fortified the outer defenses. Kashyapa moved among them, his presence a mixture of reassurance and authority.

"You have served me well," he told the soldiers, his voice carrying across the courtyard. "And now, your loyalty will be tested. Moggallana seeks to destroy what we have built. He seeks to cast us into ruin. But we will not falter. We will stand as one. Sigiriya is unbreachable, and so are we."

The soldiers cheered, their voices echoing against the stone walls. But Kashyapa could see the doubt lingering in their eyes. The omens, the whispers of curses, and the growing fear of the supernatural had taken their toll. He turned to Vihara as the crowd dispersed.

"Morale is fragile," Kashyapa said. "We must ensure the men remain steadfast. Double the patrols. Keep them busy, focused."

Vihara nodded. "As you command, Your Majesty."

---

As the sun dipped below the horizon, Kashyapa convened his council. The great hall was lit by flickering torches, casting shadows that seemed to dance with a life of their own. Varuni sat at his right hand, her expression as inscrutable as ever. Vihara stood at the far end of the table, flanked by other commanders and advisors.

"Moggallana's forces will reach us within days," Vihara reported. "We estimate three, perhaps four. They march steadily, avoiding unnecessary delays."

"And their strategy?" Kashyapa asked.

"Uncertain," Vihara admitted. "They may attempt to encircle us, cutting off supplies, or they may strike directly. Either way, they will test our defenses."

Kashyapa turned to Varuni. "You have foreseen this. What do you counsel?"

Varuni's dark eyes gleamed in the firelight. "Sigiriya is not just a fortress," she said. "It is a weapon. Use the rock's natural defenses to your advantage. The jungle is their weakness. Confuse them, divide them. Let the rock's power crush their spirit before their swords touch your walls."

Kashyapa nodded, her words igniting a spark of confidence. "Then that is what we shall do. Vihara, prepare ambushes along their approach. Slow them down. Force them to fight on our terms."

---

The next morning, the jungle came alive with activity. Vihara led a contingent of scouts and archers to lay traps along the paths leading to Sigiriya. Spiked pits were dug and camouflaged, while concealed archers took positions in the dense foliage. Kashyapa himself rode to the front lines, inspecting the preparations with a critical eye.

"They will expect a direct assault," he told Vihara. "But we will show them the cost of underestimating us. Every step they take toward this fortress will bleed them dry."

Vihara saluted. "It will be done, Your Majesty."

As Kashyapa returned to the fortress, he felt a flicker of hope. The vision from the sacred pool haunted him, but he clung to Varuni's words. Fate could be altered. The rock's power was his to command.

---

That night, as the fortress settled into an uneasy quiet, Kashyapa stood alone on the Lion Terrace. The stars above seemed distant, their light muted by the dark weight of the impending battle. He closed his eyes, seeking solace in the silence. But the silence was broken by a voice, faint and familiar.

"You cannot escape it."

Kashyapa's eyes snapped open, his hand instinctively reaching for his dagger. The terrace was empty, the shadows undisturbed. Yet the voice lingered in his mind, its tone chilling.

"The blood on your hands will drown you."

He turned sharply, scanning the darkness, but found nothing. The wind picked up, carrying with it the faint rustle of leaves and the distant cry of a night bird. Kashyapa's hand fell to his side, but his heart continued to race.

---

At dawn, the first scouts returned with reports of success. The traps had claimed their first victims, slowing Moggallana's advance. A contingent of enemy soldiers had stumbled into the pits, and the jungle's dense terrain had forced their formation to scatter.

"The rock protects us," Varuni said when Kashyapa relayed the news. "But it will test you as well. Do not falter, Your Majesty."

Kashyapa nodded, but her words carried a weight that he could not ignore. As the day wore on, preparations continued, the fortress's defenses growing ever stronger. Yet, despite the activity around him, Kashyapa felt the isolation of leadership more acutely than ever. The decisions he made in the coming days would define not only his reign but his very legacy.

As he stood once more on the Lion Terrace, watching the jungle below, Kashyapa whispered to himself: "Let them come. I will meet them, and I will prevail. Sigiriya will stand."

# CHAPTER 21: CRACKS IN THE FOUNDATION

The torchlight flickered unevenly in the great hall, casting jagged shadows on the walls as Kashyapa sat on his throne. The air felt heavier with each passing day, a suffocating weight pressing down on the court. Varuni stood by his side, her presence as enigmatic as ever, her words weaving both comfort and unease into his fraying mind.

"Your Majesty," she said, her tone measured, "the rock demands more. Its spirit must be appeased if we are to prevail against Moggallana."

Kashyapa's gaze shifted to her, his eyes bloodshot from sleepless nights. "What more can it demand, Varuni? I have given it offerings, blood, and toil. I have sacrificed all to build this fortress."

Varuni's lips curved into a faint smile. "Sacrifice is not measured by quantity, but by intent. The rock must see your unwavering devotion, your willingness to bind yourself fully to its power."

Her words hung in the air like a curse, and Kashyapa's court murmured uneasily. The nobles exchanged glances, their faces betraying their growing distrust of Varuni's influence. Whispers had already begun to circulate: Was she truly a mystic, or was she manipulating the king for her own mysterious ends?

Later that evening, Commander Vihara sought an audience with Kashyapa. He entered the throne room with a deliberate stride, his expression grim.

"Your Majesty," he began, bowing deeply. "I bring troubling news. More soldiers have deserted their posts. They fear the omens and the... occurrences. And the nobles grow restless. They question your leadership, some even murmuring of alternatives."

Kashyapa's eyes narrowed, his fingers tightening on the arms of his throne. "Alternatives?" he repeated, his voice low and dangerous.

Vihara hesitated, choosing his words carefully. "Moggallana's return has emboldened them. They see the growing unease in the court, the fear among the men. Some believe..."

"That I am weak?" Kashyapa interrupted, his voice rising. He stood abruptly, the force of his movement silencing the chamber. "They forget who sits upon this throne, who built this fortress with his own will! They forget the blood I have shed for their safety, their future."

"Your Majesty," Vihara said cautiously, "strength is not just in punishment, but in unity. If you push them too far, you risk losing their loyalty entirely."

Kashyapa glared at him, the fire in his eyes mingling with doubt. For a moment, he said nothing, his mind churning. Then he turned to Varuni.

"What do you see in this?" he asked.

Varuni stepped forward, her gaze steady. "The cracks in your foundation are real, Your Majesty, but they are not beyond repair. The spirit of Sigiriya tests you, as it tests all who serve you. Show them that their doubts are baseless. Strengthen their faith in you through decisive action."

Kashyapa's lips pressed into a thin line. "Then it shall be so. Commander, double the patrols. Any soldier caught deserting will face the harshest punishment. And as for the nobles... remind them that their loyalty is not optional."

---

The next day, Kashyapa's decrees were carried out with brutal efficiency. Guards swept through the barracks and the surrounding villages, dragging deserters back to Sigiriya in chains. The punishments were public, the executions carried out on the Lion Terrace for all to see. Blood stained the stone, and the workers below whispered of the growing darkness within the fortress.

Among the court, tensions simmered. Several nobles approached Ahalya, seeking her counsel.

"The king's actions grow more erratic," one said, his voice low and urgent. "Varuni's influence poisons his mind. If this continues, the kingdom will crumble before Moggallana even reaches our gates."

Ahalya, ever the observer, listened intently. Her own doubts had grown in recent weeks, but she knew the peril of voicing them too openly.

"The king's path is difficult," she said carefully. "But his strength has brought us this far. We must not abandon him now."

"And what of Varuni?" another noble pressed. "She speaks as if she commands the very rock itself. How much longer will we bow to her whims?"

Ahalya's silence spoke volumes, and the nobles exchanged uneasy glances. The seeds of rebellion had been sown, and it was only a matter of time before they took root.

---

Kashyapa's paranoia deepened. He began to see betrayal in every shadow, every whisper. The once-grand halls of Sigiriya felt suffocating, their walls closing in around him. Even in his dreams, he found no respite. Visions of Moggallana's army, of his own blood staining the throne, plagued him night after night.

One evening, as he paced the terrace, Varuni approached him.

"Your Majesty," she said softly, "the rock speaks to me. It warns of a great trial ahead. But it also promises strength for those who prove worthy."

Kashyapa turned to her, desperation flickering in his eyes. "What must I do?" he asked.

Varuni's gaze was unyielding. "Show them your unshakable resolve. Make a final offering to the spirit of Sigiriya. Only then will the rock's power be fully yours."

"What offering?" Kashyapa demanded.

Varuni hesitated, her expression inscrutable. "Something... precious. Something irreplaceable. Only you can decide what is worthy."

Kashyapa's mind raced, his thoughts spiraling. What could he offer that would prove his devotion? What could silence the whispers, both within the fortress and within himself?

---

That night, Kashyapa stood alone before the sacred pool, the water's surface shimmering in the torchlight. He knelt by its edge, his reflection distorted and fragmented.

"Tell me," he whispered. "What must I do to save my kingdom?"

The water remained still, offering no answers. But deep within, Kashyapa thought he saw something stir, a shadow moving just beneath the surface. Whether it was real or a product of his unraveling mind, he could not say. But the vision left him with a single, chilling thought:

The price of salvation might be more than he could bear.

# CHAPTER 22:
# AHALYA'S DILEMMA

The torches lining the inner chamber flickered uneasily, their flames casting distorted shadows across the walls. Ahalya sat at her desk, the parchment before her covered in hastily scrawled notes. Her normally steady hands trembled as she traced the names of those implicated, their connections to Dhatusena's death weaving a web of treachery that threatened to unravel everything Kashyapa had built.

She leaned back, her thoughts a chaotic swirl. The evidence she had gathered was damning, more so than she had anticipated. Several prominent nobles, including members of Kashyapa's own council, had played a role in engineering Dhatusena's downfall. Their motivations ranged from personal vendettas to ambitions of power, but their collective actions had set the kingdom on its current precarious path.

Ahalya's loyalty to Kashyapa was unwavering, but she knew that exposing this conspiracy could destabilize his reign irreparably. The court was already fractured, whispers of rebellion growing louder with each passing day. If these revelations came to light, it could push the kingdom into chaos.

As dawn broke, Ahalya stepped onto the terrace, seeking clarity in the cool morning air. Below her, the fortress buzzed with activity, soldiers and workers moving with a sense of grim determination. The sight filled her with a mixture of pride and dread. Sigiriya was Kashyapa's masterpiece, a testament to his vision and will. But it was also a powder keg, and she feared her discovery might be the spark that ignited it.

Her thoughts were interrupted by the sound of footsteps. She turned to see Commander Vihara approaching, his expression as grave as ever.

"Ahalya," he greeted, inclining his head. "You seem troubled."

She hesitated, her instinct to confide in him clashing with her fear of the consequences. Vihara had proven himself a loyal ally, but even he might struggle with the weight of her discovery.

"The court grows restless," she said finally. "The tensions between the nobles and the king are... unsettling."

Vihara's gaze hardened. "Their discontent is dangerous. But Kashyapa needs unity now more than ever. If they cannot see that, they risk dooming us all."

Ahalya nodded, her resolve firming. "I will do what I can to maintain that unity," she said, her words carefully chosen.

That evening, Ahalya returned to her chambers and carefully folded the incriminating documents, sealing them within a hidden compartment in her desk. For now, the truth would remain buried. She would protect Kashyapa's reign, even if it meant carrying the weight of this knowledge alone.

But the decision weighed heavily on her. In her dreams, she saw Sigiriya crumbling, its once-mighty walls reduced to rubble by the weight of secrets and lies. The faces of the conspirators haunted her, their smug smiles a constant reminder of their treachery.

Ahalya's internal struggle did not go unnoticed. Varuni, ever perceptive, confronted her one evening as they crossed paths in the great hall.

"You carry a burden, Ahalya," Varuni said, her tone soft but probing. "Secrets have a way of festering if left unspoken."

Ahalya stiffened, her eyes narrowing. "I do what is necessary for the good of the kingdom," she replied.

Varuni's lips curved into a faint smile. "As do we all. But remember, silence can be as dangerous as a sword. Choose your battles wisely."

The exchange left Ahalya unsettled. Varuni's words were layered with meaning, and Ahalya couldn't shake the feeling that the mystic knew more than she let on. Was Varuni an ally, or was she playing her own game, weaving herself deeper into Kashyapa's trust?

---

Meanwhile, Kashyapa continued to tighten his grip on the court. He summoned the nobles to the great hall, his voice echoing with authority as he addressed their growing unease.

"I hear your whispers," he said, his gaze sweeping over the assembled lords. "Your doubts, your fears. You question my decisions, my vision for this kingdom. But let me remind you: it is my strength that holds this kingdom together. Without it, you would all be at Moggallana's mercy."

The nobles shifted uncomfortably, some murmuring their assent while others remained silent. Kashyapa's eyes narrowed, his frustration simmering beneath the surface.

"Loyalty is not a choice," he continued. "It is a duty. And I will not tolerate disloyalty in any form. Those who stand with me will share in the glory of Sigiriya. Those who stand against me will face the consequences."

The tension in the room was palpable as Kashyapa's words hung in the air. Ahalya watched from the sidelines, her heart heavy. She could see the cracks forming in the foundation of Kashyapa's rule, but she felt powerless to stop them.

---

As the days passed, Ahalya's unease grew. She began to notice small signs of dissent among the court: furtive glances, hushed conversations, and subtle shifts in allegiance. She knew the conspiracy against Dhatusena was only the beginning. If Kashyapa did not address the underlying discontent, it would only be a matter of time before it erupted into open rebellion.

One night, unable to sleep, she returned to her desk and retrieved the hidden documents. As she read through them again, a new thought began to take shape. Perhaps the truth did not need to be a weapon of destruction. Perhaps it could be wielded as a tool of reconciliation, a way to expose the rot while preserving the kingdom.

But such a plan would require precision, trust, and the right allies. And in a court filled with shadows and secrets, allies were in short supply.

# CHAPTER 23: SHADOWS OF BETRAYAL

The moon hung high over Sigiriya, casting its silver light on the fortress's stone walls. The air was heavy with an unnatural stillness, broken only by the occasional howl of the wind. Kashyapa sat in his private chamber, his mind a storm of doubts and fears. Varuni's words from earlier that evening echoed in his ears, filling him with unease.

"Your Majesty," she had said, her voice low and deliberate, "the betrayal you fear is not distant. It lies closer than you think. Someone you trust implicitly may already be plotting against you."

Kashyapa had leaned forward, his breath catching in his throat. "Who?" he demanded.

Varuni had hesitated, her dark eyes locking onto his. "Commander Vihara," she said at last. "I have seen shadows gathering around him. His loyalty is fraying, his trust in you faltering."

The accusation gnawed at Kashyapa as he stared into the flickering flames of the brazier. Vihara had been by his side since the beginning, a steadfast ally in the chaos that had followed Dhatusena's death. Could it be true? Could his most trusted commander now harbor thoughts of betrayal?

Unable to contain his doubts, Kashyapa summoned Vihara to his chambers. The commander arrived quickly, his expression one of concern.

"Your Majesty," Vihara said, bowing low. "You requested my presence?"

Kashyapa gestured for him to rise. He studied Vihara's face carefully, searching for any hint of duplicity.

"I have heard troubling things," Kashyapa began, his voice measured but cold. "Whispers that loyalty within my court is wavering. That even among my most trusted, there are those who would see me fall."

Vihara stiffened, his brows knitting together. "Your Majesty, I have always served you faithfully. If there are those who conspire against you, I will root them out myself."

Kashyapa's gaze hardened. "And what of your own loyalty, Vihara? Can you swear to me that it remains unshaken? That you have not been swayed by doubt or ambition?"

For a moment, the room was silent save for the crackling of the fire. Vihara's eyes flashed with anger, though he quickly masked it.

"I have given my life to your cause, Your Majesty," he said evenly. "I have bled for you, fought for you, and stood by you when others fled. If my loyalty is now in question, then perhaps it is not I who have faltered."

Kashyapa's jaw tightened, the commander's words cutting deeper than he cared to admit. "Do not presume to lecture me," he said sharply. "I have enemies on all sides, and I will not hesitate to act against anyone I suspect of treachery. Not even you."

Vihara bowed his head, but his expression was grim. "I understand, Your Majesty. But I urge you to remember that fear and suspicion can destroy a kingdom faster than any army. Trust must be tempered with vigilance, but it cannot be abandoned entirely."

Kashyapa said nothing, his mind churning as Vihara left the chamber. The commander's words lingered, sowing seeds of doubt alongside the ones Varuni had planted.

---

Varuni entered shortly after Vihara's departure, her presence as steadying as it was unsettling.

"What did he say?" she asked, her tone neutral.

"He denied everything," Kashyapa replied, pacing the room. "But his words… they were calculated. Too measured. Perhaps you are right, Varuni. Perhaps he has already turned against me."

Varuni approached him, her voice soothing. "Doubt can be a powerful weapon, Your Majesty. Wield it wisely. Watch him closely, but do not act prematurely. Let him reveal himself in time."

Kashyapa nodded, though his unease remained. He had trusted Vihara with his life, and the thought of betrayal from such a close ally was almost too much to bear.

---

The following days were tense. Vihara's demeanor grew increasingly distant, his interactions with Kashyapa marked by a cool professionalism that only deepened the king's suspicions. The court, too, felt the strain, the undercurrent of mistrust spreading like a disease.

Ahalya observed the growing divide with a heavy heart. She could see the toll it was taking on both men, their once-strong bond now frayed by doubt and manipulation. She approached Vihara one evening, finding him alone in the barracks.

"Commander," she said softly, "a word, if I may."

Vihara turned to her, his expression weary. "What is it, Ahalya?"

She hesitated before speaking, choosing her words carefully. "The king… he is under immense pressure. His fears are understandable, but they cloud his judgment. He needs you now more than ever."

Vihara's lips thinned into a grim line. "I have stood by him through everything," he said. "But his trust in me is gone. How can I serve a king who no longer believes in me?"

"By proving him wrong," Ahalya replied. "By remaining steadfast, even when he falters. You are one of the few who can still reach him, Vihara. Do not let doubt destroy what you have built together."

Vihara sighed, his shoulders sagging. "I will try," he said at last. "But I fear the king is slipping further from reason with each passing day."

Meanwhile, Varuni continued to tighten her grip on Kashyapa's trust. She spoke of omens and visions, painting Vihara as a threat that could not be ignored. Her influence over the king was now absolute, her words shaping his every decision.

One night, as Kashyapa sat alone in the sacred pool chamber, Varuni approached him with a new warning.

"The spirit of the rock grows restless," she said. "It senses the fractures within your circle. If you do not act decisively, those fractures will widen, and your kingdom will crumble."

Kashyapa looked at her, his eyes shadowed with exhaustion. "And what would you have me do?" he asked.

Varuni's smile was faint but cold. "Watch, Your Majesty. Wait. And when the time comes, strike before your enemies can."

Kashyapa nodded slowly, her words a balm to his fraying nerves. But deep within, a part of him wondered if he was already too late. The shadows of betrayal were closing in, and he could no longer tell friend from foe.

# CHAPTER 24: WHISPERS IN THE FORTRESS

T he night air carried a chill through the labyrinthine halls of Sigiriya, a sharp contrast to the oppressive heat of the day. The workers huddled in their makeshift shelters, their whispered prayers barely audible over the howling wind. Rumors of Rajith's ghost had spread like wildfire, and fear gripped the fortress like a vice.

Kashyapa sat alone in the grand hall, his head heavy with exhaustion. His throne, once a symbol of his triumph, now felt like a prison. The shadows cast by the flickering torches seemed to move of their own accord, dancing across the frescoed walls. He could almost hear them whispering, though he dismissed it as a trick of the wind.

A messenger entered cautiously, his face pale. "Your Majesty," he began, his voice trembling. "The workers... they refuse to continue. They claim... they claim to hear..."

"What?" Kashyapa snapped, his patience worn thin. "Speak plainly."

The messenger swallowed hard. "They claim to hear the voice of Rajith, calling to them in the night."

Kashyapa's grip on the armrest tightened. "Nonsense," he growled. "Rajith is dead, buried beneath this fortress. His voice cannot harm us."

The messenger hesitated, then continued. "They say... they say the curse is real, Your Majesty. That his spirit seeks vengeance for his untimely death."

Kashyapa's eyes burned with anger. "Tell them that any man who refuses to work will face my wrath. Ghosts do not build fortresses—men do. Dismissed."

The messenger bowed and hurried out, his fear palpable. Kashyapa leaned back, his mind racing. The rumors were absurd, yet he could not deny the growing unrest. The air itself felt heavier, charged with an unseen force that set his nerves on edge.

---

That night, Kashyapa's sleep was fitful. He dreamed of Sigiriya's construction, the sound of hammers and chisels ringing out across the rock. But the sounds twisted, turning into anguished cries and mournful wails. He saw Rajith standing atop the Lion Terrace, his face twisted in anger. Blood dripped from his hands, staining the pristine stone beneath him.

"You cannot bury the truth," Rajith's ghost intoned, his voice echoing like thunder. "This fortress will be your tomb."

Kashyapa woke with a start, his chest heaving. The room was dark, save for the faint glow of the moon through the high windows. He rubbed his eyes, dismissing the dream as a product of his own guilt. Yet the unease lingered, a shadow that refused to be banished.

---

The next morning, Kashyapa summoned Varuni. The mystic entered with her usual composure, her dark eyes observing him closely.

"You look troubled, Your Majesty," she said.

Kashyapa hesitated before speaking. "The workers speak of

103

Rajith's ghost. They claim to hear his voice at night, and now... I have seen him in my dreams. What is happening, Varuni? Has the curse truly taken hold?"

Varuni's expression did not waver. "The spirit of Sigiriya is powerful," she said. "It demands balance. Rajith's death was a disruption, a wound that has not healed. You must appease the rock, Your Majesty. Only then will the whispers cease."

"And how am I to do that?" Kashyapa demanded. "What more can it ask of me?"

Varuni stepped closer, her voice dropping to a near-whisper. "A final offering. Something precious. Something irreplaceable. The rock must know your devotion is absolute."

Kashyapa's stomach churned. He had already given so much. What more could he offer? The thought filled him with dread, yet he could not ignore Varuni's words. The visions, the whispers —they were not mere coincidences. The fortress itself seemed alive, its spirit entwined with his own fate.

---

As the sun set, the fortress was bathed in an eerie red light, the horizon ablaze with the colors of dusk. Kashyapa stood atop the Lion Terrace, gazing out over the jungle below. The workers had resumed their tasks under threat of punishment, but their movements were slow, their fear palpable.

"Rajith's ghost," he muttered to himself. "Is it truly him, or is it my own guilt given form?"

Behind him, Ahalya approached cautiously. "Your Majesty," she said softly, "you should rest. The weight you carry is too great for one man."

Kashyapa turned to her, his eyes weary. "Rest? How can I rest when my own fortress conspires against me? When the dead refuse to stay buried?"

Ahalya hesitated, then placed a hand on his arm. "You are not alone, Your Majesty. There are those who still believe in you, who still stand by your side. Do not let fear consume you."

Her words offered a fleeting comfort, but Kashyapa knew the path ahead would not be easy. The whispers in the fortress grew louder with each passing night, and the visions of Rajith became more vivid. The line between reality and nightmare blurred, leaving Kashyapa to wonder if he was losing his grip on both his kingdom and his sanity.

That night, Kashyapa returned to the sacred pool. The water's surface was still, reflecting the dim torchlight. He knelt by its edge, his reflection staring back at him with haunted eyes.

"If this is my fate," he whispered, "then so be it. But I will not fall without a fight."

The water rippled, though there was no wind. For a moment, Kashyapa thought he saw Rajith's face staring back at him, a cruel smile playing on his lips. He blinked, and the image was gone, replaced by his own reflection. Yet the unease remained, a constant reminder that the past was not so easily buried.

As he rose to leave, a voice—low and mournful—seemed to echo through the chamber. "You cannot escape what you have done."

Kashyapa froze, his blood running cold. He turned sharply, but the chamber was empty. The voice, whether real or imagined, lingered in his mind as he made his way back to his chambers, his resolve hardening.

Sigiriya would stand, no matter the cost. And if Rajith's ghost sought to undermine him, then Kashyapa would face him—even if it meant confronting the darkest corners of his own soul.

# CHAPTER 25: THE OMINOUS ECLIPSE

The sky turned an ominous shade of gray, a foreboding shroud that blanketed the kingdom. Even the birds grew silent, their usual chatter replaced by an eerie stillness. Kashyapa stood atop the Lion Terrace, his gaze fixed on the heavens as the sun began its slow descent into shadow. The eclipse was not unexpected, but its arrival seemed to unearth fears long buried within the hearts of his people.

Below, the fortress bustled with frantic activity. Soldiers and workers alike hurried to complete the latest round of fortifications Kashyapa had ordered. Sigiriya, already a marvel of engineering, was transforming into an impenetrable citadel. Yet even its towering walls and hidden tunnels did little to quell the unease that had settled over the kingdom.

Varuni appeared at Kashyapa's side, her movements as fluid as the shadows that danced across the terrace.

"It is a sign, Your Majesty," she said softly. "The heavens mirror the chaos within your kingdom. The spirit of Sigiriya grows restless, and Moggallana draws near."

Kashyapa's jaw tightened, his hands gripping the stone railing. "Then we must be ready," he said. "No matter what omens the sky delivers, Sigiriya will stand. Moggallana will find nothing but defeat here."

Varuni inclined her head, her dark eyes gleaming. "Preparation is wise, Your Majesty. But do not ignore the warnings. The eclipse is more than a celestial event. It is a call to action, a reminder that time grows short."

The court convened later that day, the chamber filled with tension as Kashyapa outlined his latest orders.

"New defenses will be added to Sigiriya," he declared. "The gates will be reinforced with iron, and additional traps will be installed within the tunnels. I want the water gardens converted into barriers. If Moggallana's forces breach our walls, they will find nothing but death awaiting them."

The nobles exchanged uneasy glances. Commander Vihara, standing at the edge of the chamber, stepped forward.

"Your Majesty," he began, his voice steady but cautious. "The soldiers are already stretched thin. To implement these new defenses, we will need to conscript more workers from the surrounding villages. This will not sit well with the people."

Kashyapa's eyes narrowed. "The people will do what is necessary to protect their king and their kingdom. If they refuse, remind them of the consequences of disloyalty."

Vihara hesitated, his jaw tightening. "As you command, Your Majesty."

Ahalya, seated near the back of the chamber, watched the exchange with growing concern. Kashyapa's resolve was undeniable, but his increasing reliance on fear and coercion was eroding the very foundations of his rule. She made a mental note to speak with Vihara privately, hoping to find a way to temper the king's escalating demands.

As the eclipse reached its zenith, the kingdom plunged into an unnatural darkness. The streets of the villages below were eerily quiet, the people huddled in their homes, whispering prayers to ward off the ill omen. Even within Sigiriya, the soldiers' movements grew hesitant, their usual bravado tempered by the weight of superstition.

Kashyapa paced the Lion Terrace, his mind racing. The fortress was his masterpiece, his legacy. Yet no matter how high he built its walls, he could not shake the feeling that something greater —something beyond his control—was closing in.

Varuni's voice echoed in his mind. "The spirit of Sigiriya grows restless." What did it mean? Was the rock itself turning against him, or was it merely his own guilt and paranoia given form?

---

That night, Kashyapa called for Varuni in the sacred pool chamber. The flickering torchlight reflected off the water's surface, casting an otherworldly glow. When Varuni arrived, she found him staring into the pool, his expression grim.

"The eclipse has shaken my people," he said without turning. "And it has unsettled me as well. What must I do to ensure victory, Varuni? What does the spirit demand of me?"

Varuni stepped closer, her presence calm and unyielding. "You must show the spirit that your will is stronger than any force that seeks to destroy you. Sacrifices have been made, but the ultimate test is yet to come. When the time arrives, you will know what must be done."

Kashyapa's fists clenched at his sides. "Cryptic words and half-truths will not save this kingdom, Varuni. Speak plainly."

For the first time, Varuni's composure faltered, a flicker of unease crossing her face. "The spirit speaks in riddles, Your Majesty. But it has shown me glimpses of the future. Moggallana's arrival is inevitable. And when he comes, you must face him not just as a king, but as a man unafraid to confront his own demons."

Kashyapa turned to her, his expression hard. "Then I will be ready. Whatever it takes, I will not let this kingdom fall."

---

In the days that followed, the fortress buzzed with renewed urgency. Workers toiled from dawn until dusk, their efforts driven as much by fear as by loyalty. Kashyapa oversaw every detail, his presence a constant reminder of the stakes.

Yet beneath the surface, discontent simmered. The nobles grumbled about the king's heavy-handed tactics, while the soldiers' morale continued to erode. Whispers of rebellion grew louder, their echoes reaching even the most guarded corners of the court.

Ahalya, ever vigilant, began to piece together the threads of a brewing conspiracy. She saw the way certain nobles lingered in hushed conversations, their glances filled with distrust. She knew that if Kashyapa's rule was to survive, the fractures within the kingdom would need to be addressed—and soon.

---

As the eclipse faded and the sun's light returned, Kashyapa stood atop the fortress, surveying the land below. The jungle stretched endlessly in all directions, a sea of green that seemed both protective and suffocating. Somewhere beyond its borders, Moggallana was gathering his forces, preparing to strike.

Kashyapa's grip on the railing tightened. Sigiriya was not just a fortress; it was a symbol of his reign, his defiance, and his ambition. He would not let it fall. But as the shadows of the eclipse lingered in his mind, he could not shake the feeling that the true battle would be fought not with swords and shields, but within his own soul.

# CHAPTER 26: THE TRIAL OF VIHARA

The sun dipped low over Sigiriya, painting the fortress in hues of crimson and gold, as if the heavens themselves bore witness to the unfolding strife within its walls. The great hall buzzed with a restless energy, the courtiers' faces drawn with unease. Rumors had spread like wildfire—Commander Vihara, the king's trusted ally, now stood accused of treason.

Kashyapa sat upon his throne, his expression as cold and unyielding as the stone beneath him. In his hand, he clutched a series of messages—forged, though he did not yet know it—that painted Vihara as a conspirator with Moggallana. The damning words on the parchments had been slipped into his chamber during the night, their origins unclear but their implications devastating.

Varuni stood at his side, her presence both a comfort and a reminder of the shadows that had grown around him. She had urged caution but agreed the matter could not be ignored. Kashyapa's court was rife with suspicion, and any hint of betrayal demanded swift action.

Vihara was brought forward, his hands bound but his head held high. His armor had been stripped, leaving him vulnerable in the eyes of those who once followed his commands. He met Kashyapa's gaze without flinching.

"Your Majesty," he said, his voice steady despite the murmurs that rippled through the hall. "I stand accused, yet I do not know my crime. What evidence condemns me?"

Kashyapa's eyes burned with a mixture of anger and sorrow. "These letters," he said, holding up the parchments. "Messages intercepted from a courier. They bear your seal, Vihara, and speak of plans to aid Moggallana in his assault on this kingdom."

A gasp ran through the hall. Vihara's jaw tightened, his eyes narrowing. "Your Majesty, these letters are forgeries. I have sworn my life to you and this kingdom. I would never betray you."

"And yet they exist," Kashyapa countered. "Their presence alone casts doubt upon your loyalty. Can you prove they are false?"

Vihara's silence spoke volumes. He had no means to disprove the accusations, no way to uncover the perpetrator behind the forgery. The court's whispers grew louder, the nobles exchanging glances that ranged from pity to satisfaction.

Varuni stepped forward, her voice cutting through the noise. "Your Majesty, the spirit of Sigiriya grows restless. It demands justice, but also caution. A trial will reveal the truth. Let the commander speak his defense before the gods and his peers."

Kashyapa hesitated, his hands gripping the armrests of his throne. Finally, he nodded. "Very well. Vihara, you will stand trial. The court shall decide your fate."

The trial was held the following morning, the great hall transformed into an arena of judgment. Vihara stood at its center, surrounded by nobles and soldiers whose expressions betrayed their divided loyalties. Ahalya watched from the sidelines, her heart heavy. She had long suspected that forces within the court sought to undermine Kashyapa, and now they had succeeded in driving a wedge between him and his most loyal ally.

As the evidence was presented, Vihara maintained his innocence. He spoke of his years of service, his sacrifices, and his unwavering dedication to Kashyapa's vision. But the forged letters loomed over him, their damning words impossible to refute.

"Your Majesty," Vihara said, turning to Kashyapa. "I have followed you into battle. I have defended this kingdom with my life. If you truly believe I am guilty, then let my execution serve as proof of your resolve. But know this—your enemies are not those who stand before you, but those who hide in the shadows, feeding on your doubt."

Kashyapa's expression flickered, a momentary crack in his steely demeanor. But the court's eyes were upon him, and he could not afford to show weakness.

"The evidence is clear," he said at last, his voice heavy. "Commander Vihara, you are found guilty of treason. You will be imprisoned until further notice. Let this serve as a warning to all who would conspire against me."

Ahalya's breath caught in her throat. The sentence was not as severe as she had feared, but it was no less devastating. As Vihara was led away, his head still held high, she resolved to uncover the truth behind the letters. The kingdom's survival depended on it.

In the days that followed, the fortress grew more tense. The soldiers, many of whom had served under Vihara, were demoralized. The nobles whispered among themselves, their loyalties fracturing further. Kashyapa roamed the halls like a restless spirit, his guilt and paranoia gnawing at him.

"You did what was necessary," Varuni told him one evening as they stood in the sacred pool chamber. "The spirit of Sigiriya demands strength. Any sign of weakness would have emboldened your enemies."

Kashyapa nodded, but her words did little to ease his turmoil. Vihara's final statement lingered in his mind: *Your enemies are not those who stand before you, but those who hide in the shadows.*

Ahalya worked tirelessly, poring over documents and questioning servants in secret. She discovered inconsistencies in the letters, small details that suggested they had been crafted by someone intimately familiar with Vihara's habits and handwriting. Her investigation led her to a nobleman named Mahendra, whose sudden rise in influence coincided with the arrival of the letters.

Confronting him, however, would be dangerous. Mahendra had powerful allies, and any accusation without proof could backfire. Ahalya knew she would need to tread carefully if she hoped to clear Vihara's name and expose the true traitors within the court.

As night fell over Sigiriya, Kashyapa stood atop the Lion Terrace, his gaze fixed on the horizon. The jungle stretched out before him, dark and impenetrable. Somewhere beyond its borders, Moggallana's army was gathering, preparing to strike.

"The walls are closing in," Kashyapa murmured to himself. "The shadows grow deeper, and I can no longer see the light."

Behind him, Varuni appeared, her presence as silent as ever. "The spirit tests you, Your Majesty," she said. "But you are strong. You will endure."

Kashyapa turned to her, his expression unreadable. "Will I?" he asked. "Or have I already lost?"

Varuni's smile was faint but confident. "The spirit does not choose the weak, Your Majesty. Trust in its will. And trust in yourself."

But as Kashyapa stared out into the darkness, he could not shake the feeling that his kingdom, and his soul, were slipping through his fingers.

# CHAPTER 27: THE LAST RITUAL

The chamber beneath Sigiriya was dimly lit, its air thick with the scent of burning herbs and incense. Varuni stood at the center, her silhouette illuminated by the flickering light of oil lamps. Around her, an intricate pattern of runes had been etched into the stone floor, their meaning ancient and unknowable. Kashyapa hesitated at the entrance, his steps heavy as he approached.

"You summoned me," Kashyapa said, his voice steady but tinged with weariness.

Varuni turned, her eyes gleaming with a fervor that unnerved him. "The time has come, Your Majesty. The spirit of Sigiriya demands a final offering."

Kashyapa's gaze swept over the room, taking in the ceremonial altar and the tools arranged meticulously upon it. "I have given enough," he said. "My people have suffered. My court is fractured. What more could it possibly want?"

Varuni stepped closer, her movements deliberate. "This fortress was built on blood and ambition. It stands as a testament to your will, but the spirit that binds it requires balance. A part of you must be offered—a symbolic sacrifice to seal your place as Sigiriya's rightful ruler."

Kashyapa's jaw tightened. "You speak in riddles, Varuni. What are you asking of me?"

She gestured to the altar, where a ceremonial dagger lay. Its blade glinted ominously in the lamplight. "A piece of your essence, Your Majesty. Be it your blood, your dreams, or something more profound. Only then can the fortress's spirit be pacified."

The room grew silent as Kashyapa considered her words. His mind raced with doubt and defiance. Memories of his ascent to power flashed before him—the coup, his father's death, the betrayal of those he once trusted. All of it had led to this moment.

"No," he said finally, his voice firm. "I will not submit to some unseen force. Sigiriya stands because of my vision, my strength. It owes me, not the other way around."

Varuni's expression darkened, her calm demeanor giving way to something more intense. "You misunderstand, Your Majesty. The spirit does not bargain. If you refuse, the balance will shatter, and everything you have built will crumble. Do not let pride blind you to the cost of defiance."

Kashyapa stepped forward, his presence imposing despite the tension in the air. "I have faced betrayal, war, and the weight of my own sins. I will not let superstition dictate my fate. This is my kingdom, and I alone will determine its destiny."

Varuni's lips pressed into a thin line, but she said nothing more. Instead, she stepped aside, allowing Kashyapa to leave the chamber. As he ascended the spiral staircase back into the fortress, a sense of foreboding settled over him. The air felt heavier, the walls seeming to close in as if the fortress itself disapproved of his decision.

Above, the court was alive with activity. Soldiers prepared for the looming threat of Moggallana's forces, while nobles whispered in hushed tones. Ahalya caught sight of Kashyapa as he emerged from the shadows, her eyes searching his face for any sign of clarity.

"Your Majesty," she said, approaching cautiously. "The soldiers are readying for battle, but morale is low. They need reassurance."

Kashyapa nodded, his expression unreadable. "They will have it. Call a gathering at the Lion Terrace. I will address them myself."

That evening, Kashyapa stood before his assembled forces, the wind carrying his words across the terrace. He spoke of resilience, of the strength that had carried them through every trial. He reminded them of Sigiriya's grandeur, its walls a testament to their shared determination.

"This fortress is more than stone and mortar," he declared. "It is our legacy. And no enemy, no shadow from the past, will take it from us. Stand with me, and together we will ensure that Sigiriya endures for generations to come."

The soldiers cheered, their voices rising in unison. For a moment, Kashyapa felt a flicker of hope. But as the crowd dispersed, leaving him alone on the terrace, the weight of Varuni's warning returned.

That night, Kashyapa dreamed of the fortress crumbling around him. The walls cracked and splintered, the rock itself seeming to roar with anger. Amid the chaos, he saw Varuni standing amidst the rubble, her eyes glowing with an otherworldly light.

"You cannot defy the spirit," she said, her voice echoing. "It will take what it is owed."

Kashyapa awoke with a start, his chest heaving. The chamber was dark, save for the faint glow of the moon through the high windows. He rose from his bed, his mind churning with questions. Was Varuni's warning a manipulation, or was there truth in her words? Could Sigiriya's spirit truly turn against him?

As dawn broke, Kashyapa stood at the edge of the Lion Terrace, gazing out over the jungle. The horizon was shrouded in mist, the landscape both beautiful and foreboding. He clenched his fists, his resolve hardening.

"Whatever comes," he muttered, "I will face it. This is my kingdom. My throne."

But deep within the fortress, the spirit of Sigiriya stirred, its presence growing stronger with each passing moment. And though Kashyapa refused to see it, the cracks in his foundation—both literal and figurative—were beginning to show.

# CHAPTER 28:
# THE GHOST OF
# DHATUSENA

A storm raged over Sigiriya, lightning illuminating the fortress in bursts of pale fire. The torrential rain struck the stone walls like a relentless drumbeat, as though the heavens themselves sought to test Kashyapa's resolve. Alone in his chamber, he paced, his mind burdened by Varuni's cryptic warnings and the looming threat of Moggallana's forces.

Each flash of lightning revealed his reflection in the polished bronze mirror on the far wall. His face was drawn, his eyes shadowed with fatigue and something deeper: guilt. Despite his attempts to bury it, the memory of his father's death resurfaced with cruel clarity. The room seemed colder, the storm's howl echoing like a dirge.

Suddenly, the torches flickered, their flames shrinking as if a great wind had swept through the chamber. But no windows were open. Kashyapa froze, his hand instinctively reaching for the dagger at his side. The air grew heavy, oppressive, and the temperature plummeted.

"Kashyapa," a voice rasped, low and filled with accusation.

He turned sharply, his heart pounding. There, in the corner

of the chamber, stood a figure cloaked in shadows. Lightning illuminated the face of his father, King Dhatusena. The apparition's features were gaunt, its eyes hollow yet burning with an unnatural light.

"Father?" Kashyapa whispered, his voice trembling. "This cannot be."

The ghost stepped closer, its movements slow and deliberate. "You dishonor our blood," it said, its tone devoid of warmth. "You betrayed me. You betrayed your brother. And now, you betray this kingdom with your hubris."

Kashyapa's grip tightened on his dagger. "I did what I had to," he said, his voice rising. "You left me no choice. You favored Moggallana, cast me aside as if I were nothing."

"And what have you gained?" Dhatusena's ghost hissed. "A fortress built on fear? A throne stained with blood? You sought power, but it will destroy you."

Kashyapa's jaw clenched. "I am king! Sigiriya is my legacy, a symbol of my strength. The people will remember my name long after the storms have passed."

The ghost's expression twisted into something almost pitiable. "They will remember, but not as you hope. Moggallana approaches, and your fortress will not save you. The spirits of this land do not recognize your rule, Kashyapa. They demand justice."

Another crack of lightning illuminated the chamber, and the apparition vanished. Kashyapa staggered, his breath coming in short, ragged gasps. He sank onto the edge of his bed, his dagger slipping from his hand and clattering to the floor.

---

The storm continued to rage as Kashyapa sat in silence, the ghost's words echoing in his mind. He had seen many strange things since the construction of Sigiriya began—visions, omens, shadows that moved without cause—but this was different. This was personal.

He rose and made his way to the sacred pool chamber, where he knew Varuni would be. She was there, as expected, her hands tracing the runes etched into the stone walls. She looked up as he entered, her expression unreadable.

"You've seen something," she said, her voice calm but firm.

Kashyapa nodded, his hands trembling despite himself. "My father. He appeared to me. He spoke of betrayal, of the spirits rejecting my rule. What does it mean, Varuni? Am I cursed?"

Varuni stepped closer, her dark eyes searching his face. "The spirits are restless," she said. "They sense the imbalance in your soul. Your guilt, your fear—these are cracks in the foundation of your reign. You must confront them if you are to survive what is to come."

Kashyapa's expression hardened. "I have no time for riddles. Moggallana is on the march. My people need a king who is strong, unshaken."

"Strength does not come from denial," Varuni said, her tone sharp. "It comes from understanding your weaknesses and overcoming them. If you do not face the truth, the spirits will not stand with you when the final battle arrives."

The following morning, Kashyapa stood before his council, his demeanor more composed but his mind still haunted by the vision. He ordered additional fortifications to be constructed and the soldiers to double their training. Every detail was scrutinized, every potential weakness addressed.

Yet beneath the surface, his paranoia deepened. He questioned the loyalty of his nobles, his generals, even his servants. Every shadow seemed to hold a threat, every whispered conversation a conspiracy.

Ahalya, observing his behavior, grew increasingly concerned. She approached Commander Vihara, who had been released from imprisonment but remained under watch.

"The king is unraveling," she said quietly. "If we do not find a way to restore his faith in himself and those around him, he will lead us all to ruin."

Vihara nodded, his expression grim. "I will speak with the soldiers. Their loyalty may be the key to stabilizing him. But we must tread carefully. Kashyapa trusts no one now."

That night, Kashyapa returned to the Lion Terrace, where the storm had left the air thick with the scent of rain. The jungle stretched before him, dark and foreboding. Somewhere beyond the horizon, Moggallana was preparing his assault.

"Father," Kashyapa murmured to the wind, "I will not fall as you did. Sigiriya will not fall. This kingdom is mine, and I will protect it. Whatever it takes."

But as the wind howled through the trees and the fortress's walls, it seemed to carry a whisper, low and mournful:

*Justice will come.*

# CHAPTER 29: MOGGALLANA'S ARRIVAL

The dawn broke with an ominous stillness, as if the jungle surrounding Sigiriya itself held its breath in anticipation. Scouts returned to the fortress at first light, their faces grim and their horses lathered with sweat. Moggallana's army was no longer a distant threat; it was marching steadily toward Sigiriya, a wave of inevitability that no barrier could hold back forever.

In the great hall, Kashyapa convened his council. The atmosphere was charged with tension, the air thick with unspoken fears. Varuni stood at his side, silent and watchful, her enigmatic presence a source of both comfort and unease.

"Speak," Kashyapa commanded, his voice cutting through the murmurs. "What is the state of their forces?"

A scout stepped forward, his head bowed. "Your Majesty, Moggallana's army is vast. Thousands of soldiers, war elephants, siege engines. They march with precision, and their intent is clear. They mean to take Sigiriya."

Kashyapa's gaze hardened, his jaw tightening. "Let them come. Sigiriya was built to withstand any assault. We will show them the strength of this fortress and the will of its king."

The nobles exchanged uneasy glances. Commander Vihara, reinstated but still under scrutiny, spoke cautiously. "Your Majesty, the soldiers are loyal, but morale is low. The rumors of curses and betrayals have sown doubt. They need reassurance, a sign that we stand united."

Kashyapa rose from his throne, his presence commanding. "Then I will give them that sign. Prepare the troops for my address. Let them see their king and know that we fight not just for a fortress, but for our legacy."

---

By midday, the soldiers had assembled on the Lion Terrace, their ranks stretching out beneath the shadow of Sigiriya's towering rock. The sight was both inspiring and daunting, a reminder of the scale of the battle to come. Kashyapa stood before them, clad in ceremonial armor that gleamed in the sunlight.

"Men of Sigiriya," he began, his voice carrying over the gathered ranks. "Our enemies march upon us, their hearts filled with the hope of our defeat. But they do not know what we are capable of. They do not know the strength of this fortress, the strength of its people."

He paced along the terrace, meeting the eyes of his soldiers. "Sigiriya is more than stone and mortar. It is a testament to our resilience, our vision, and our unity. We will show Moggallana that no force, no army, can break us. Together, we will ensure that our legacy endures."

The soldiers roared their approval, their cheers echoing off the rock face. For a moment, the doubts and fears that had plagued them seemed to dissipate, replaced by a collective resolve.

---

As preparations for the battle intensified, Varuni sought out Kashyapa in the sacred pool chamber. The room was dimly lit, the still water reflecting the flickering flames of the torches. She approached him cautiously, her expression grave.

"Your Majesty," she said, her voice low. "The spirit has spoken to me one last time. It offers a final prophecy."

Kashyapa turned to her, his brow furrowing. "What does it say?"

Varuni hesitated, choosing her words carefully. "Your blood will stain the throne, but your legacy will endure. The spirit sees your name written in the annals of history, but at a cost. The choice remains yours, but the outcome cannot be altered."

Kashyapa's expression darkened. "More riddles. More half-truths. I have no use for cryptic warnings, Varuni. Tell me plainly—what must I do?"

"Lead your people," she said simply. "Face your brother. The spirit's will is not to guide you, but to remind you that every action has a consequence. You cannot escape fate, but you can shape how it is remembered."

Kashyapa clenched his fists, his frustration evident. "I will not fall. This throne, this kingdom, belongs to me. Moggallana will find nothing but defeat at our gates."

Varuni inclined her head, her expression inscrutable. "Then may the spirit grant you strength, Your Majesty."

---

As night fell, the fortress buzzed with activity. Soldiers sharpened their weapons, artisans reinforced the walls, and scouts monitored the enemy's progress. Kashyapa walked among them, offering words of encouragement and inspecting the defenses. Despite his outward confidence, the weight of Varuni's prophecy lingered in his mind.

In the privacy of his chamber, Kashyapa unrolled a map of the surrounding terrain. Vihara joined him, their discussion focused on strategy.

"We have the advantage of height and fortifications," Vihara said. "But Moggallana's numbers cannot be underestimated. If they breach the outer defenses, the battle will become far more dangerous."

"They won't breach them," Kashyapa said firmly. "Sigiriya will hold."

Vihara hesitated before speaking again. "Your Majesty, if the prophecy is true—"

"Enough," Kashyapa interrupted, his tone sharp. "I will not base my decisions on whispers and visions. We fight with strategy, with strength, not with fear."

Vihara nodded, though his unease was palpable. "As you command, Your Majesty."

---

By the time the first light of dawn crept over the horizon, Moggallana's army was visible in the distance, their banners dark against the sky. Kashyapa stood atop the fortress walls, his gaze fixed on the approaching threat. Behind him, Sigiriya's soldiers took their positions, their determination bolstered by their king's presence.

The final battle was at hand, and with it, the culmination of Kashyapa's ambition and legacy. The spirits of Sigiriya watched in silence, their judgment looming as inevitable as the clash to come.

# CHAPTER 30: THE CALM BEFORE THE STORM

The sun rose over the jungle surrounding Sigiriya, casting a golden glow over the fortress. Yet, for all its beauty, the day felt foreboding. The stillness of the morning air was heavy, as if the land itself braced for the impending clash. Kashyapa stood on the Lion Terrace, gazing out at the horizon where Moggallana's forces had encamped. The distant banners rippled in the wind, a silent reminder of the challenge that loomed.

In the solitude of the terrace, Kashyapa's thoughts turned inward. His reflection stared back at him in the still waters of the sacred pool, the lines of his face etched deeper than he remembered. The weight of his choices pressed on him: the betrayal of his father, the rise to power through bloodshed, and the endless paranoia that had consumed his reign. For a moment, he wondered if it was all worth it—the throne, the fortress, the legacy.

Footsteps broke his reverie, and Ahalya's voice followed. "Your Majesty," she said softly, her tone hesitant.

He turned to her, his expression unreadable. "What is it, Ahalya?

Speak your mind."

Ahalya hesitated, clutching a scroll in her hands. "I have uncovered something. About your father's death. About those who conspired against him."

Kashyapa's eyes narrowed. "Conspired? You mean it was not just my actions that led to his fall?"

"No," she said, her voice steady now. "Certain nobles, those closest to the throne, orchestrated his betrayal. They manipulated events, knowing it would drive you to act. They sought to weaken the kingdom for their own gain."

Kashyapa took the scroll from her hands, his gaze scanning the words. Names leapt out at him, names of men who still held positions of power in his court. His fists clenched as anger flared within him.

"Why bring this to me now?" he demanded. "Why wait until the enemy is at our gates?"

Ahalya's expression was pained. "I feared what this knowledge might do to you, Your Majesty. But now, with Moggallana so near, I thought you should know the truth."

Kashyapa's laughter was bitter. "The truth? The truth is a luxury we can no longer afford. My focus must be on the battle ahead, not on the treachery of the past." He handed the scroll back to her. "Seal this away. We will deal with it after we secure victory."

As the day wore on, the tension in the fortress grew palpable. Soldiers sharpened their weapons and fortified their positions, while messengers moved swiftly between the walls. Kashyapa's generals gathered in the war room, poring over maps and strategizing for the inevitable siege. Commander Vihara—his loyalty still questioned by many—stood firm, his experience invaluable despite the doubts surrounding him.

"Their main force will target the western wall," Vihara said, pointing to the map. "It's the most vulnerable point, though it's heavily defended. We should station our best archers here."

Kashyapa nodded. "And the eastern approach? Could they use it as a feint?"

"Unlikely, but we cannot leave it unguarded," Vihara replied. "A small contingent should be enough to hold it."

The king's gaze lingered on the map, his mind working through the possibilities. "Very well. Ensure the soldiers are ready by nightfall. Dismissed."

As the generals filed out, Kashyapa remained, staring at the map as if it held answers to questions he dared not voice. He felt Varuni's presence before she spoke, her footsteps soft against the stone floor.

"You waver," she said, her voice a mix of observation and reproach.

"I do not waver," Kashyapa replied, though his tone betrayed him. "I prepare."

"Preparation is meaningless if your spirit is divided," Varuni said. "You carry the weight of too many ghosts, Your Majesty. You must let them go."

Kashyapa turned to face her, his expression defiant. "And how would you have me do that? By performing more of your rituals? By bowing to the whims of unseen forces?"

Varuni's eyes hardened. "By accepting that the throne is not just a seat of power, but a seat of responsibility. Your people look to you not as a man, but as their protector. Whatever ghosts haunt you, they must not see them."

---

That evening, Kashyapa addressed his troops one final time. Torches lined the terrace, their flames casting long shadows across the stone walls. The soldiers stood in silence, their faces resolute as their king spoke.

"Tomorrow, we face our greatest test," Kashyapa said, his voice steady. "Moggallana comes not just for this fortress, but for everything we have built. He seeks to destroy our legacy, to erase our names from history."

He paused, letting his words sink in. "But we will not fall. We will stand together, as one people, as one kingdom. Sigiriya is our home, our pride, and we will defend it with all that we have."

The soldiers cheered, their voices rising in unison. For a moment, the doubts and fears that had plagued them seemed to fade, replaced by a collective determination.

As the fortress settled into an uneasy quiet, Kashyapa returned to his chamber. The weight of the coming battle pressed on him, yet his mind was oddly calm. He thought of his father, of Moggallana, of the choices that had brought him here.

"Tomorrow," he murmured to himself, "the storm will break. And with it, the truth of my reign will be revealed."

Outside, the jungle was alive with the sounds of night. The wind whispered through the trees, carrying with it the faint scent of rain. In the distance, Moggallana's campfires dotted the horizon like fallen stars, their glow a reminder of the battle to come.

The calm before the storm had ended. Tomorrow, the fate of Sigiriya would be decided.

# CHAPTER 31: THE SIEGE BEGINS

As the first rays of dawn kissed the fortress of Sigiriya, the horizon came alive with the relentless march of Moggallana's army. The jungle's serene canopy swayed ominously in the morning breeze, its tranquility shattered by the rhythmic drumbeats of war. Sigiriya stood resolute against the rising tide, its towering rock a symbol of defiance and Kashyapa's unyielding resolve.

From the summit, Kashyapa surveyed the encroaching forces. Moggallana's army was a sea of banners and armor, their numbers seemingly endless. War elephants trumpeted in the distance, their handlers guiding them with calculated precision. Behind them, siege engines loomed, their menacing shadows a promise of destruction.

"They're testing our resolve," Commander Vihara said, joining Kashyapa on the balcony. His voice was calm but laced with tension.

"Let them test," Kashyapa replied, his gaze unflinching. "They will find Sigiriya more formidable than they imagined."

The first skirmish came at midday. Moggallana's archers launched a volley of flaming arrows, aiming for the outer defenses. Kashyapa's soldiers responded swiftly, extinguishing the flames and returning fire. Stones hurled from the fortress's catapults crashed into the advancing lines, scattering men and crushing siege ladders.

"Hold the line!" Vihara shouted, his command rippling through the ranks. The soldiers obeyed, their determination bolstered by their leader's unwavering presence.

On the western wall, where the assault was fiercest, Kashyapa himself appeared, rallying his troops. His golden armor gleamed in the sunlight, a beacon of strength amidst the chaos. The sight of their king inspired the defenders, who fought with renewed vigor, pushing back the invaders.

---

As night fell, the battlefield grew eerily silent. Fires burned in the distance, their smoke curling into the starless sky. Kashyapa convened his council in the war chamber, the air heavy with the day's toll.

"Casualties?" Kashyapa asked, his voice clipped.

"Minimal, Your Majesty," Vihara replied. "But they've only tested our defenses. The real assault is yet to come."

"Supplies?"

"Enough for now," said Ahalya, who had been overseeing logistics. "But if this siege drags on, we'll face shortages."

Kashyapa nodded, his expression unreadable. "Then we must ensure it doesn't drag on. Vihara, increase patrols on the eastern wall. If Moggallana plans a feint, that's where it will be. Ahalya, see to the wounded. Morale must remain high."

---

The second day brought new challenges. Moggallana's forces began constructing trenches and battering rams, their intentions clear. Kashyapa's engineers worked tirelessly to reinforce the gates, their efforts driven by the king's insistence on unyielding defenses.

In the midst of this, whispers of unease spread among

the soldiers. Tales of the fortress's curse resurfaced, fueled by strange occurrences: tools inexplicably breaking, shadows moving where none should be, and the faint sound of whispers carried on the wind.

Varuni approached Kashyapa in the sacred pool chamber, her expression grave. "The spirits are restless, Your Majesty. They sense the bloodshed to come."

"Let them be restless," Kashyapa said, his tone dismissive. "Their whispers will not breach these walls."

"But their influence can," Varuni warned. "The men's fears grow, and fear is a weapon Moggallana can wield."

Kashyapa frowned, but he did not reply. Instead, he turned his attention back to the map before him, his mind racing with strategies.

---

By the third day, Moggallana's army launched a full-scale assault. Siege towers rolled toward the walls, their iron-bound frames impervious to arrows. Soldiers swarmed the western gate, their battering ram pounding relentlessly.

"Bring the oil!" Vihara commanded. Barrels of boiling oil were hauled to the parapets and poured onto the attackers, their screams echoing across the battlefield.

On the eastern wall, a contingent of Moggallana's troops attempted to scale the cliffs, hoping to exploit the weaker defenses. Kashyapa anticipated the move and stationed his best marksmen there. The cliffs became a death trap, arrows raining down on the invaders and sending them plummeting to their deaths.

---

As dusk fell, the battlefield was littered with the bodies of the fallen. The air was thick with the stench of blood and smoke, and the cries of the wounded pierced the night. Kashyapa walked among his soldiers, offering words of encouragement and inspecting the defenses.

"You fought well today," he told a group of archers, their faces streaked with soot and sweat. "Rest now, for tomorrow we fight again."

Despite his words, Kashyapa's mind was heavy with doubt. The siege was taking its toll, and he knew that time was not on their side. Supplies dwindled, and the soldiers' resolve, though strong, began to waver.

In the privacy of his chamber, Kashyapa stared out at the jungle, the flickering lights of Moggallana's camp taunting him. He thought of Varuni's warnings, of the curse that seemed to shadow his every move. For the first time, he wondered if Sigiriya's grandeur was not a testament to his power, but a monument to his hubris.

---

The night brought no solace. As Kashyapa tried to sleep, his dreams were plagued by visions of Dhatusena and Rajith. Their faces were pale, their eyes accusing.

"You built your throne on the blood of the innocent," Dhatusena's ghost said. "And now that blood calls for vengeance."

Rajith's voice followed, a whisper that cut like a blade. "The foundation of Sigiriya is cracked, Kashyapa. And when it falls, so will you."

Kashyapa woke with a start, his chest heaving. He rose from his bed and walked to the balcony, the cool night air doing little to calm him. In the distance, the sound of drums echoed, a reminder that the siege's end was far from near.

"Let them come," he murmured to himself, gripping the stone railing. "Sigiriya will endure. I will endure."

But even as he spoke the words, a shadow of doubt lingered in his heart.

# CHAPTER 32: THE FINAL PROPHECY

The storm that had loomed on the horizon for days finally broke over Sigiriya. Rain lashed the fortress, hammering against its stone walls and pooling in the intricately carved steps. The jungle below was a blur of swaying trees and surging winds. In the throne room, Kashyapa stood before Varuni, her presence as ominous as the tempest outside.

"The spirits are restless," Varuni began, her voice carrying an unnatural weight. "They sense what is to come."

Kashyapa's jaw tightened. He had grown weary of her cryptic warnings. "Spare me your riddles, Varuni. Speak plainly."

She stepped closer, her dark eyes piercing. "You cannot win this battle, Kashyapa. The omens are clear. Moggallana's army is not merely a force of men—it is destiny itself bearing down upon you. If you continue to resist, Sigiriya will fall, and your blood will stain its stones."

The king's hand gripped the hilt of his sword. "You dare suggest surrender?" His voice was low, dangerous.

"I suggest survival," Varuni countered. "There is still a way to preserve your legacy. Surrender the throne to Moggallana. Step aside and let the bloodshed end."

Kashyapa's laugh was bitter, echoing through the chamber. "Step aside? After all I have sacrificed? After all I have built?" He gestured to the walls around him. "Sigiriya is my legacy! It is my throne, my monument! I will not bow to the man who fled our land like a coward."

Varuni's gaze did not waver. "Your refusal to bend will break you, Kashyapa. The spirits have shown me your end. I have seen the blood, the despair, the fall."

The words hung in the air like a curse. Kashyapa's grip tightened, his knuckles white. "Enough," he said, his voice cold. "You speak of betrayal cloaked in prophecy. Perhaps it is you who conspires against me. Perhaps it is your whispers that weaken my men."

Varuni's expression hardened. "You are blind, Kashyapa. Blind to the truth, blind to the path that could save you. I have served you faithfully, but I will not stand idly by as you destroy yourself and this kingdom."

"Then leave," Kashyapa snapped, his voice rising. "Leave and take your omens with you. I need no spirits to tell me what I already know. Victory is mine to claim, and I will not falter."

Varuni lingered for a moment, her eyes searching his face. Finally, she turned and walked away, her footsteps echoing in the vast hall. "You will remember these words," she said over her shoulder. "And when the end comes, you will know that it was not fate that brought you down, but your own pride."

---

The rain continued to pour as Kashyapa descended to the war room. His generals awaited him, their faces tense. Maps and reports lay scattered across the table, marked with the movements of Moggallana's forces.

"What is the status of the western defenses?" Kashyapa asked, his tone brusque.

"Holding, but barely," Vihara replied. "Their siege engines are relentless. We can't sustain this pace for much longer."

"Then we must strike before they breach," Kashyapa said. "Prepare a sortie. Hit their supply lines under the cover of this storm. We will remind Moggallana that Sigiriya is no easy prize."

The generals exchanged uneasy glances. Finally, Ahalya spoke. "Your Majesty, the men are weary. Morale is low. A bold strike could rally them, but it could also cost us dearly if it fails."

"It will not fail," Kashyapa said firmly. "Vihara, you will lead the attack. Take our swiftest riders and our most skilled archers. Strike hard and fast, and return before dawn."

Vihara hesitated, then nodded. "As you command, Your Majesty."

As preparations for the sortie began, Kashyapa returned to the sacred pool. The water was turbulent, disturbed by the storm's vibrations. He knelt beside it, his reflection distorted by the ripples.

"Father," he murmured, his voice barely audible. "If you can hear me, if you watch from whatever realm you now dwell in, know that I do this for our name. For our legacy."

The pool seemed to respond, the ripples converging into a single point. For a brief moment, Kashyapa thought he saw a face in the water—Dhatusena's face, stern and sorrowful. He blinked, and the vision was gone.

That night, the sortie rode out under the cover of darkness. Rain masked their movements, and for a time, it seemed they might succeed. The western camp of Moggallana's forces was caught off guard, their supplies set ablaze.

But as the raiders began their retreat, disaster struck. Moggallana had anticipated such a move and laid an ambush. Vihara and his men found themselves surrounded, their escape cut off.

Kashyapa watched from the summit as distant flames and sounds of battle filled the night. His chest tightened with dread. "Signal them to retreat," he ordered, though he knew it was too late.

The morning revealed the grim aftermath. The sortie had failed, and Vihara was among the captured. Moggallana sent a message with his prisoners: surrender, or face annihilation.

Kashyapa's hands trembled as he read the message. He crushed the parchment and threw it into the fire. "Prepare the defenses," he said to his remaining generals. "We fight to the last."

The storm raged on, but inside Sigiriya, a greater storm brewed. Kashyapa's resolve was unshaken, but the cracks in his foundation grew wider. The final battle loomed, and with it, the reckoning of his reign.

# CHAPTER 33: THE BATTLE BEGINS

T he first light of dawn crept over Sigiriya, casting long shadows across the fortress and the jungle below. The calm morning belied the chaos that was about to unfold. From the summit, Kashyapa watched Moggallana's forces gather, their banners rippling in the wind, their formations precise and intimidating.

"Let them come," Kashyapa muttered under his breath, gripping the hilt of his sword. "Sigiriya will not fall."

The tension in the air was palpable as Kashyapa descended to the courtyard, where his generals awaited him. Their faces bore a mixture of determination and dread. Asu, Kashyapa's second in command, stood at attention, his expression unreadable.

"They march," Asu said curtly. "Their advance is steady. Siege engines are being deployed at the eastern flank."

Kashyapa nodded. "We will meet them with fire and stone. Archers, ready your positions. I want every boulder rolled into place. No weakness in our defense."

Ahalya stepped forward, her voice quiet but firm. "Your Majesty, the soldiers are afraid. Whispers of curses and apparitions have spread. They need reassurance—a sign that their king still commands the gods' favor."

"The gods favor those who seize victory with their own hands," Kashyapa snapped, but he caught the doubt in Ahalya's eyes. He softened his tone. "I will address them."

Moments later, Kashyapa stood atop the western wall, the soldiers below gazing up at him with wary eyes. He raised his arms, his voice ringing out over the tumult of preparations.

"Brave warriors of Sigiriya! Today, we defend not just these walls, but the honor of our kingdom and the legacy of our ancestors. The enemy may think they have the gods on their side, but the gods dwell here, within this sacred fortress! Look around you. These stones, this rock, this throne—it is our divine shield. Stand firm, and let no man, no force, no spirit break your resolve!"

A cheer rose from the ranks, hesitant at first but growing louder. Kashyapa stepped down, his expression unreadable.

As the sun climbed higher, Moggallana's army advanced. The thunder of war drums echoed through the jungle, followed by the metallic clatter of siege engines. Boulders hurled by trebuchets crashed against the walls, shaking the fortress to its core.

Kashyapa's archers retaliated, their arrows raining down in deadly arcs. Firepots were hurled from the walls, exploding among the enemy ranks in bursts of flame and smoke. For a time, the defenders held their ground, their spirits bolstered by Kashyapa's speech.

But then the supernatural began.

It started with the shadows. As the battle raged, dark, indistinct figures appeared among the rocks surrounding the fortress. At first, they seemed like illusions, tricks of the light. But the soldiers' fear grew as the shadows moved against the grain of the sunlight, their forms unnatural and unearthly.

"What are those?" a soldier gasped, his bow trembling in his hands.

"Hold your ground!" Asu barked, but even his voice betrayed a hint of unease.

The eerie sounds came next. Low, mournful wails carried on the wind, rising and falling like the cries of tortured souls. The sounds seemed to emanate from the very walls of Sigiriya, chilling the soldiers to their cores.

Kashyapa's fists clenched as he stood atop the central tower, watching his forces falter. He turned to Varuni, who had appeared at his side as if summoned by the chaos.

"Is this your doing?" he demanded, his voice low and dangerous.

Varuni's expression was calm, but her eyes glinted with something unreadable. "The spirits are restless, Your Majesty. They demand tribute."

"There has been enough tribute!" Kashyapa roared. "Enough blood spilled for their insatiable hunger!"

Varuni tilted her head, her voice a whisper. "Then you must face them, as only a true king can."

---

The battle intensified as Moggallana's forces breached the first layer of defenses. The outer walls, weakened by years of neglect and the relentless siege, crumbled under the assault. Kashyapa's soldiers fell back to the inner sanctum, their numbers dwindling.

Amid the chaos, Ahalya approached Kashyapa, her face pale but resolute. "Your Majesty, the time has come to use the secret tunnels. If we can lead a contingent behind enemy lines..."

Kashyapa shook his head. "No. This is our stronghold. We hold here or we die here."

"If you fall, the kingdom falls," Ahalya insisted. "Please, Your Majesty, consider—"

"Enough," Kashyapa said, his voice cold. "I will not abandon

Sigiriya."

As the day wore on, the supernatural phenomena grew more intense. Fires erupted inexplicably within the fortress, spreading panic among the defenders. The shadows became more distinct, their forms resembling the long-dead workers who had perished during Sigiriya's construction. Their hollow eyes seemed to judge Kashyapa as he strode through the corridors, issuing commands.

By nightfall, the fortress was a battlefield of both physical and spiritual conflict. Kashyapa stood at the heart of it all, his sword drawn, his resolve unbroken despite the horrors surrounding him.

The final assault was imminent, and Kashyapa knew the moment of reckoning had arrived. He turned to Asu, who stood bloodied but unbowed at his side.

"Gather the remaining forces," Kashyapa said. "We make our stand here."

Asu nodded, his loyalty unwavering despite everything. "For Sigiriya."

"For Sigiriya," Kashyapa echoed, his voice steady. But as he looked out over the battlefield, he could not shake the feeling that the spirits of Sigiriya—and perhaps even his own father —were watching, waiting for the final chapter of his story to unfold.

# CHAPTER 34: THE VISION UNFOLDS

The first light of dawn pierced through the smoky haze hanging over the battlefield. From his vantage point atop Sigiriya, Kashyapa observed the chaos below. The enemy's siege engines had pushed closer during the night, their relentless assault breaking through sections of the outer walls. Yet it was not the sight of his enemy's progress that sent a chill through his veins—it was the uneasy silence among his own ranks.

The air was heavy with an ominous tension, as though the jungle itself held its breath. Kashyapa's war elephant, a majestic beast bedecked in golden armor, stood restless at the center of the remaining forces. The animal, named Yajni, had been Kashyapa's companion through many battles, a living symbol of his power. Today, Yajni seemed unnaturally agitated, swaying and trumpeting softly as if sensing the weight of impending doom.

Varuni's words echoed in Kashyapa's mind: *Your blood will stain the throne, but your legacy will endure.* He clenched his fists, forcing himself to dismiss the prophecy. Fate was for the weak. He would carve his destiny with his own hands.

As the enemy forces surged closer, Kashyapa descended to the courtyard to rally his troops. The soldiers looked to him with a mixture of desperation and hope, their spirits frayed by days of relentless siege and eerie phenomena. The haunting cries that had echoed through the fortress the night before were fresh in their minds.

Kashyapa mounted Yajni, raising his sword high. "Today, we end this!" he bellowed. "Moggallana thinks he can take what is ours, but he underestimates the strength of Sigiriya! We fight for our land, our families, and our future. Let the world remember this day as the day Sigiriya stood unbroken!"

A ragged cheer rose from the ranks, and for a brief moment, Kashyapa felt a surge of confidence. He signaled for the gates to open, and his forces poured out to meet the enemy in a final, desperate charge.

---

The battlefield was a maelstrom of sound and movement. Spears clashed against shields, arrows darkened the sky, and the ground trembled under the weight of advancing troops. Kashyapa led the charge atop Yajni, cutting through enemy lines with calculated precision. His golden armor gleamed in the sunlight, a beacon for his soldiers to rally around.

But then, the vision began to unfold.

Yajni, normally steady and fearless, suddenly reared up, trumpeting loudly. Kashyapa struggled to control the beast as it twisted and turned, its eyes wide with panic. The soldiers around him hesitated, their momentum faltering as they watched their king's symbol of power spiral into chaos.

From the corner of his eye, Kashyapa saw the shadowy figures again. They moved through the enemy ranks, indistinct yet terrifying, their presence sowing confusion and fear. The cries of the supernatural mingled with the clamor of battle, and the line between reality and nightmare blurred.

"Hold your ground!" Kashyapa shouted, but his voice was

drowned out by the roar of the battlefield and Yajni's panicked trumpeting.

---

The retreat began subtly at first. A few soldiers, spooked by the shadows and the elephant's distress, began to pull back. Their movement rippled through the ranks like a contagion. What started as a minor withdrawal quickly escalated into a full-scale retreat as panic spread.

Kashyapa's heart sank as he realized what was happening. "No!" he roared, driving Yajni forward in a desperate attempt to rally his forces. "Do not turn your backs! Stand and fight!"

But it was too late. The soldiers, convinced the battle was lost, fled toward the fortress, abandoning their positions. Moggallana's forces seized the opportunity, pressing their advantage with ruthless efficiency.

Amid the chaos, Yajni stumbled and fell, throwing Kashyapa to the ground. He landed hard, the impact jolting him but leaving him uninjured. As he scrambled to his feet, he found himself surrounded by enemy soldiers. Their faces were grim, their weapons raised.

Kashyapa's grip tightened on his sword. If this was how it ended, he would die fighting. But before he could strike, a horn sounded from the enemy lines, signaling a pause. The soldiers hesitated, stepping back as Moggallana himself approached.

---

The brothers faced each other for the first time in years, their eyes locking across the battlefield. Moggallana, clad in simple yet commanding armor, exuded a quiet confidence. His gaze was steady, devoid of hatred, yet resolute.

"Brother," Moggallana said, his voice carrying over the din. "This need not end in bloodshed. Surrender, and I will spare your life."

Kashyapa's laugh was bitter, hollow. "Surrender? To you? The coward who fled to India and plotted against his own blood? Never."

"Your pride blinds you," Moggallana replied. "Look around you. Your soldiers have abandoned you. Sigiriya has fallen. Do not let more lives be lost for the sake of your vanity."

Kashyapa raised his sword, his voice defiant. "Sigiriya has not fallen. As long as I draw breath, this land remains mine."

Moggallana's expression hardened. "So be it." He raised his hand, signaling his soldiers to advance.

---

The battle resumed with renewed ferocity, but Kashyapa knew the tide had turned irrevocably. His forces were scattered, his fortress breached, and the prophecy was on the verge of fulfillment. Yet even in the face of defeat, he fought with the desperation of a man who refused to bow to fate.

As the sun dipped below the horizon, casting the battlefield in shadows, Kashyapa found himself pushed back toward the fortress gates. His golden armor was tarnished, his sword arm heavy, but his spirit remained unbroken.

"This is not the end," he whispered to himself, his eyes blazing with determination. "Sigiriya will remember."

# CHAPTER 35: VARUNI'S FINAL WORDS

The battlefield below Sigiriya was a cacophony of chaos and despair. Moggallana's forces surged with unrelenting ferocity, pressing closer to the fortress walls. Kashyapa, watching from a high parapet, gripped the edge with white-knuckled hands. The golden hues of sunset bathed the scene in an eerie glow, casting long shadows that seemed to crawl toward him, accusing and inevitable.

Varuni entered the chamber behind him, her presence as commanding as ever. She moved with quiet determination, her robes flowing like liquid dusk. Kashyapa turned to face her, his expression a mask of defiance.

"You were wrong," he said, his voice sharp and bitter. "Sigiriya will not fall. I will not fall."

Varuni's eyes softened, but her words carried the weight of unyielding truth. "The spirits are restless, my king. You have pushed against the tides of fate for too long. Even now, they whisper of your downfall."

"Spirits?" Kashyapa's laughter was hollow, echoing against the stone walls. "Do they fight with swords and shields? Do they command armies? No, Varuni. This is a battle of men, not of whispers and shadows."

"You are blind to what is before you," she replied. "The visions, the omens, the curse—you have seen their power, yet you deny it. This is your final chance. Surrender, and your blood need not stain the throne."

Kashyapa's hand moved instinctively to the hilt of his sword. "You speak of surrender as if it is salvation. But I know better. To surrender is to admit weakness, to cede the legacy I have fought so hard to build." He stepped closer to her, his voice dropping to a dangerous whisper. "You are the one who fails to see. Sigiriya is my destiny, my monument to immortality. I will not bow to my brother. I will not bow to fate."

Varuni's gaze did not falter. "You mistake stubbornness for strength, Kashyapa. The spirits will not be denied. Your refusal to heed their warnings has brought us to this brink."

The air between them grew heavy with tension. Outside, the sounds of battle grew louder. The gates of Sigiriya creaked under the strain of Moggallana's battering rams. Kashyapa's soldiers fought valiantly, but the tide was turning against them.

"You think me weak," Kashyapa said, his voice low and trembling with anger. "But it is you who has betrayed me with your riddles and half-truths. You have poisoned the minds of my court and my people with your prophecies of doom. You have undermined my reign."

Varuni's expression darkened. "I have served only the truth. It is not my doing that you have chosen to ignore it."

Kashyapa's eyes blazed with fury. "Leave. You are no longer welcome here. Take your warnings and your curses and vanish from my sight."

For a moment, Varuni hesitated, her features softening with something like pity. Then she straightened, her voice calm but resolute. "Very well, my king. I will go. But know this: the spirits will have their due, with or without my help."

With that, she turned and walked away, her figure disappearing into the dim corridors of the fortress. Kashyapa watched her go, a mixture of relief and unease settling over him. For the first time, he felt truly alone.

As the battle raged on, Kashyapa descended to the lower levels of the fortress. The air was thick with smoke and the cries of the wounded. Soldiers looked to him with desperate eyes, their faith wavering. He mounted a war elephant—not Yajni, who had fallen in the earlier chaos, but a younger, untested beast.

"We will hold the line," he declared to his commanders. "Sigiriya has withstood greater threats than this. Remember who you fight for. Remember what we defend."

The commanders nodded, their faces grim. But as Kashyapa rode into the fray, he could not shake the memory of Varuni's final words. The spirits will have their due. The phrase echoed in his mind, intertwining with the sounds of clashing steel and the screams of the dying.

By nightfall, the situation had grown dire. Moggallana's forces had breached the outer defenses, and the once-impenetrable fortress of Sigiriya now seemed vulnerable. Kashyapa fought with the ferocity of a cornered lion, cutting down enemies with a skill and precision born of desperation. Yet even his strength could not turn the tide.

As the moon rose high above the battlefield, casting its pale light over the carnage, Kashyapa found himself surrounded. His remaining soldiers formed a protective circle around him, their expressions a mixture of loyalty and resignation.

"My king," one of his commanders said, his voice trembling, "we cannot hold them off much longer. Perhaps it is time to consider —"

"No," Kashyapa interrupted, his voice ironclad. "Sigiriya will not fall. I will fight to my last breath."

And so, with the odds stacked against him and the shadows of prophecy closing in, Kashyapa prepared to make his final stand. The spirits, the curses, the betrayals—none of it mattered now. All that mattered was the legacy he would leave behind.

The night stretched on, the fortress trembling under the weight of its king's defiance. And in the distance, the faint sound of a drumbeat began to rise, as if the jungle itself was preparing to bear witness to the end of an era.

# CHAPTER 36: THE COLLAPSE

Smoke rose from the lower defenses, now reduced to rubble under Moggallana's relentless assault. The once-unyielding fortress was now a crumbling monument to a king's hubris.

Kashyapa stood at the summit, his figure silhouetted against the fiery horizon. His armor was battered, his sword stained with blood, yet he held himself tall. Around him, his remaining loyal soldiers awaited orders, their eyes heavy with despair.

"We fight to the last," Kashyapa declared, his voice steady despite the chaos below. "Sigiriya is not just stone and mortar; it is the soul of this kingdom. If we fall, we do so as warriors, not cowards."

The soldiers nodded, though their spirits wavered. Moggallana's forces, emboldened by their victories, surged closer, scaling the walls and overwhelming what remained of Kashyapa's defenses. The cries of battle echoed through the jungle, blending with the mournful calls of distant birds.

---

Inside the fortress, Kashyapa retreated to the throne room, seeking a moment of solitude. The chamber, once a symbol of his power, now felt like a tomb. The frescoes that adorned the walls seemed to mock him, their painted figures frozen in eternal celebration while his world crumbled.

A shadow moved across the room. Kashyapa turned sharply, his hand instinctively gripping his sword. But it was not an intruder. The shadow coalesced into the familiar figure of Dhatusena, his father, standing with an expression of cold disapproval.

"You have brought this upon yourself," the apparition said, its voice resonating with an otherworldly timbre. "Your greed, your betrayal, your refusal to heed the warnings. This is your legacy."

Kashyapa's chest tightened, but he refused to look away. "I did what I had to do to secure this kingdom," he replied. "Everything I did was for my people, for their future."

"Your people?" Dhatusena's voice grew colder. "Look outside. See the ruin you have wrought. This is not their future; it is their damnation."

The vision dissolved, leaving Kashyapa alone once more. But the weight of his father's words lingered, cutting deeper than any blade.

# CHAPTER 37: THE KING'S LAST STAND

The summit of Sigiriya loomed under a blood-red sky, the sun casting its final rays upon the fortress that had once been Kashyapa's symbol of divine rule. Now, it was a monument to his undoing. The cacophony of battle had subsided, leaving only the crackle of distant fires and the anguished cries of the fallen. Kashyapa stood at the edge of the summit, his once-mighty frame now bowed by the weight of defeat.

The winds howled around him, carrying whispers from the past—a thousand voices accusing, mourning, and warning. Kashyapa's armor, dented and smeared with blood, clinked faintly as he moved. He clutched his sword, the blade heavy in his hand, not from its weight but from the burden of his choices. He gazed out at the battlefield below, where Moggallana's forces celebrated their hard-won victory. The banners of the usurper—his brother—fluttered defiantly in the breeze.

"It was always meant to end this way, wasn't it?" Kashyapa murmured, his voice hoarse. The rock beneath his feet seemed to pulse with a life of its own, as if the ancient spirits of Sigiriya were alive, watching, judging.

Behind him, a figure emerged from the shadows. It was

Dhatusena, or the ghostly semblance of the man Kashyapa had betrayed. The former king's spectral presence was both ethereal and menacing, his face a mask of sorrow and fury.

"You sought immortality," Dhatusena said, his voice a low, resonant echo. "But all you have achieved is infamy."

Kashyapa turned slowly, meeting the ghost's unrelenting gaze. "You denied me the legacy I deserved," he replied, his words trembling with a mix of defiance and regret. "I built this fortress to defy the heavens, to claim my destiny. Was that not enough?"

Dhatusena's eyes burned like embers. "Legacy is not built on blood and betrayal. You poisoned the roots of your reign the moment you betrayed your family."

Memories surged forward, unbidden and vivid. The day he had sealed Dhatusena within the walls, the architect's body buried in the foundations, and the countless lives sacrificed to bring his vision to life. Each act of ambition now felt like a shackle around his soul. Kashyapa sank to his knees, his sword clattering to the stone.

"Was I wrong?" he whispered. "Was it all for nothing?"

"You already know the answer," Dhatusena's voice softened, tinged with a sorrow that cut deeper than any accusation. "The question is, what will you do now?"

Kashyapa's mind swirled with doubt and despair. The sacred pool's vision had come to pass: the retreating elephant, the collapsing army, the final humiliation. He had tried to defy fate, but every step had only brought him closer to the inevitable. And now, he stood alone, stripped of allies, of power, of purpose.

He rose unsteadily, turning back toward the edge of the summit. Below, the jungle stretched endlessly, a reminder of the natural world's indifference to human ambition.

Varuni's voice echoed in his mind. "Your blood will stain the throne, but your legacy will endure." What legacy could there be in this ruin?

Footsteps echoed behind him. He turned sharply, expecting

153

another ghost, another specter of his guilt. Instead, it was Ahalya, breathless and tear-streaked, clutching a scroll in her hands.

"My king," she said, her voice trembling. "I have proof... proof of the conspiracy against Dhatusena. It wasn't you who..." Her words faltered as she took in the desolation on his face.

Kashyapa's gaze softened, and for a moment, a flicker of the man he once was shone through. "It no longer matters, Ahalya," he said gently. "The truth will not change what I have done. It cannot erase the blood on my hands."

"But it can change how you are remembered," she pleaded. "Let the people know you were not the monster they think you are."

He smiled faintly, a weary, broken smile. "History will weave its own tale, Ahalya. My time is over."

He stepped closer to the edge, the wind whipping around him, tugging at his cloak. Ahalya's eyes widened in alarm. "My king, please..."

He raised a hand, silencing her. **"Tell them I fought for a dream. Tell them I sought to carve a place among the gods. And tell them... I failed."**

With one final breath he stepped forward, into the void.

Ahalya's scream pierced the silence, but it was swallowed by the wind. The rock seemed to shudder as if mourning its king. The ghost of Dhatusena lingered for a moment longer before dissolving into the air, leaving only the whisper of his words: "Legacy is not in monuments, but in the lives we touch."

As the sun dipped below the horizon, Sigiriya stood silent and still, a towering grave to the ambition and tragedy of a fallen king.

# CHAPTER 38:
# MOGGALLANA'S
# VICTORY

**M**oggallana stood at the base of Sigiriya, the towering fortress now wrapped in a heavy, unnatural silence. The vibrant murals and shimmering gardens that once defined the grandeur of this citadel were now scarred by the fires of battle. Broken weapons littered the ground, and the bodies of soldiers—his own and Kashyapa's—lay scattered like offerings to an unyielding god. The air was thick with smoke and the metallic tang of blood, a grim testament to the final clash of brothers.

He ascended the winding pathways toward the summit, each step resonating with the weight of what had been lost. Sigiriya, the symbol of Kashyapa's ambition, loomed above like a monolith of defiance and despair. As Moggallana climbed higher, the jungle's cacophony faded, replaced by an oppressive stillness that seemed to seep from the rock itself.

At the summit, Moggallana found the remnants of Kashyapa's final stand. The bloodied ground marked the spot where the self-proclaimed god-king had fallen. His golden armor, tarnished and dented, lay discarded nearby, while his sword—a once-glorious weapon—was half-buried in the dirt, its blade dulled and lifeless. Moggallana knelt and ran his fingers over the hilt, a pang of sorrow cutting through the triumph in his heart. Kashyapa had been his brother, a boy who had once laughed and shared dreams beneath the same royal canopy. Now, he was a cautionary tale of ambition untethered by morality.

Turning his gaze to the horizon, Moggallana saw the sprawling jungle stretching endlessly, the land their father had once ruled with wisdom and restraint. His generals and advisors approached cautiously, their expressions a mix of reverence and unease. They knew better than to interrupt the moment of victory—and its accompanying grief.

"The fortress is ours, my king," said Commander Parinda, bowing low. "Kashyapa's forces have either fled or surrendered. Sigiriya is...yours."

Moggallana nodded but did not turn. His voice, when it came, was quiet yet firm. "No," he said, the single word hanging heavily in the air. "Sigiriya belongs to the dead. It belongs to Kashyapa and the ghosts he created here. It will not be mine."

The gathered men exchanged uncertain glances, but none dared question the king's declaration. Moggallana's gaze swept over the intricate frescoes adorning the rock's walls, their colors dimmed by soot yet still hauntingly vivid. The women painted there seemed to watch him, their enigmatic smiles as inscrutable as the land's ancient spirits.

"This place is cursed," he continued. "Whatever glory Kashyapa sought to forge here is stained by blood and betrayal. We will leave it as it is—a monument to his hubris and a warning to those who dare defy the will of the gods."

Parinda hesitated. "And...what of the fortress, my king? Should we not—"

"No," Moggallana interrupted sharply. His tone brooked no argument. "Let Sigiriya stand as it is. We will not inhabit it, nor shall we tear it down. Let the jungle reclaim it, as it was always meant to."

A murmur of assent rippled through the group, though unease lingered in their eyes. Moggallana turned to face them fully, his expression hardened. "The people need a ruler who will rebuild what has been broken. They need peace. And peace does not dwell here."

He descended the summit, leaving the summit's eerie stillness behind. As he walked, the memories of his brother's laughter echoed faintly in his mind. Kashyapa had been more than a rival; he had been a reflection of the darkness that power could bring. For all his faults, Kashyapa had dared to dream, and that audacity would forever mark Sigiriya as a place of tragic beauty.

As Moggallana returned to the gathered troops, he raised his voice to address them. "We march back to Anuradhapura," he declared. "There, we will restore what was lost. But let Sigiriya remain a reminder. Tell its story so that our children will know the cost of pride."

The soldiers cheered, though it was a subdued victory cry, tempered by the weight of their king's words. As they prepared to leave, Moggallana cast one last look at the towering rock. The sun was setting behind it, casting long shadows that seemed to stretch like grasping fingers. In that moment, Sigiriya was both magnificent and forlorn, a symbol of the fleeting nature of power and the enduring scars of ambition.

When the soldiers finally departed, the jungle crept closer, its vines and foliage beginning to reclaim the stone pathways. The whispers of Sigiriya's ghosts lingered in the air, carried on the wind that swept through the now-empty fortress. It would stand for centuries, a silent witness to the rise and fall of kings, its secrets buried beneath layers of time and myth.

For Moggallana, the victory was bittersweet. He had reclaimed his father's throne, but the price had been steep—the loss of his brother, the taint of civil war, and the haunting legacy of Sigiriya. As the jungle's shadows swallowed the last remnants of the day, Moggallana's heart was heavy with the knowledge that, in many ways, no one had truly won.

Sigiriya stood eternal, a testament to human ambition and the price it demands.

# CHAPTER 39:
# AHALYA'S RECORD

As the golden hues of the setting sun bathed Sigiriya's summit in an ethereal light, Ahalya sat alone in the remnants of Kashyapa's court. Her parchment lay unrolled before her, the ink poised in her trembling hand. The fortress was silent now, save for the distant calls of the jungle—a solemn requiem for the fallen king and the chaos he had left behind.

Ahalya's thoughts churned as she recalled the last moments of Kashyapa's reign. Her quill hovered over the page, its blank expanse both a challenge and an opportunity. Would she write of the man who sought to defy the gods and fate, or of the king who succumbed to his own demons?

She dipped the quill into the ink and began.

*Kashyapa, the Lion King of Sigiriya, was a figure both revered and reviled. To his followers, he was the architect of a golden age, the visionary who transformed an isolated rock into an unparalleled masterpiece. To his detractors, he was a usurper, a patricide, and a man driven mad by ambition and paranoia.*

But history, Ahalya knew, was never so simple.

Her words carried the weight of truth and the necessity of omission. She recalled how Kashyapa's charisma had once held the court together, his speeches igniting hope in even the most doubtful hearts. Yet beneath his commanding presence lurked a man haunted by the shadow of his father, Dhatusena. Kashyapa's ascent had been tainted from the start, his throne built on treachery and blood.

The memory of his death lingered vividly. Alone atop the summit, with the echoes of Moggallana's victory resounding below, Kashyapa had confronted the ghosts of his past. His final act, one of defiance and despair, spoke to the duality of his soul. Was he a victim of fate, or had he authored his own doom?

Ahalya hesitated, her quill pausing mid-sentence. She had uncovered truths during her time in the court—truths that could alter the narrative forever. There were whispers of conspiracies among the nobles, their secret machinations nudging Kashyapa toward his fall. And then there were the supernatural occurrences: the visions of Rajith, the unearthly sounds that had plagued the fortress, and Varuni's cryptic prophecies. Writing of these would invite skepticism, even derision. Yet to omit them felt like a betrayal of the very essence of Kashyapa's story.

*The spirits of Sigiriya were restless, their presence a constant in the fortress's final days. The workers spoke of Rajith's ghost wandering the halls, while Kashyapa himself admitted to seeing visions of his father. Were these mere fabrications of a paranoid mind, or was Sigiriya truly cursed? Even now, as I write, the air feels charged with an otherworldly energy, as if the rock itself mourns its king.*

Ahalya's script flowed, weaving a tale of triumph, hubris, and inevitable tragedy. She recounted Kashyapa's descent into paranoia, his increasing reliance on Varuni's guidance, and his eventual alienation of those closest to him. The trial of Vihara, the imprisonment of dissenting nobles, and the final battle with

Moggallana all painted a picture of a man at war with both his enemies and himself.

But as she wrote, Ahalya chose to soften certain edges. She omitted the names of the nobles who had plotted against Kashyapa, instead attributing his downfall to broader forces of fate and ambition. She minimized the more grotesque aspects of his rituals, presenting them as acts of devotion rather than desperation. And while she acknowledged Varuni's influence, she refrained from delving too deeply into her role in Kashyapa's decisions.

*Kashyapa's legacy is not one of simple condemnation or celebration. He was a man who dared to dream beyond the limitations of his time, yet he was also a man undone by the weight of his aspirations. Sigiriya stands as both his triumph and his tomb, a testament to what is possible when human ambition reaches for the heavens, and a cautionary tale of what happens when it oversteps its bounds.*

The fortress, now abandoned by royal decree, would soon be reclaimed by the jungle. Moggallana had declared it cursed, his soldiers refusing to set foot within its walls. The vibrant frescoes and intricate water gardens would fade, their splendor reduced to mere whispers in the annals of history. But Ahalya's record would endure, preserved in the hope that future generations might understand the complexities of Kashyapa's life and reign.

She set down her quill and reread her work. The words captured the man she had known, the king who had inspired and terrified her in equal measure. But more importantly, they captured the essence of Sigiriya itself—a place of wonder and dread, a monument to the fragile line between greatness and ruin.

Ahalya rolled the parchment carefully, sealing it with wax. As she placed it into a leather satchel, she cast one last glance at the summit. The sun had dipped below the horizon, leaving the rock shrouded in twilight. The air was heavy, as if the earth itself mourned the passing of its lion-hearted king.

"May your story be told," she whispered, her voice barely audible against the rising wind. With that, she turned and descended the stone steps, leaving Sigiriya and its ghosts behind.

# CHAPTER 40: THE ABANDONMENT OF SIGIRIYA

Ahalya wandered through the abandoned corridors, her heart heavy with conflicting emotions. She had remained behind to chronicle the final days of Kashyapa's reign, but the weight of her task seemed insurmountable. Each fresco, each engraved stone told a story of a dream that had turned into a nightmare.

In the central chamber, she paused before a mural depicting Kashyapa in all his glory. His painted visage radiated power and determination, yet now it seemed a cruel mockery of the man who had met such a tragic end. Ahalya's hand trembled as she traced the outline of his face.

"History will remember you as a tyrant," she murmured, her voice breaking. "But I will ensure it also remembers your humanity."

A sudden gust of wind swept through the chamber, extinguishing her lantern. In the darkness, she felt a presence— not threatening, but solemn. Gathering her resolve, she relit the flame and continued her work, determined to preserve the truth as she had witnessed it.

Weeks turned into months, and Sigiriya stood deserted. The jungle, relentless and unyielding, began reclaiming the fortress. Vines crept over the stone walls, and wildflowers sprouted in the once-manicured gardens. The pools that had mirrored the skies now reflected a chaotic tangle of foliage.

Travelers passing by would often stop to gaze at the towering rock, now shrouded in mystery. Stories of Kashyapa's fall spread far and wide, evolving into legend. Some spoke of the cursed king whose ambition defied the gods, while others revered him as a visionary undone by betrayal. The truth, like the fortress itself, lay hidden beneath layers of time and myth.

In the capital, Moggallana's reign began to take shape. He restored the old city and focused on rebuilding the kingdom, his efforts driven by a desire to distance himself from his brother's legacy. Yet, despite his success, he could not escape the shadow of Sigiriya. The people whispered of the "Cursed Rock," and its memory lingered like an unspoken warning.

One evening, as Moggallana sat in his chambers, Ayodhya approached with a scroll. "Your Majesty, Ahalya has completed her record of Kashyapa's reign. She wishes for your approval before it is presented to the court."

Moggallana took the scroll, his fingers brushing against the rough parchment. He unrolled it and began reading, his expression unreadable. Ahalya's words were vivid, capturing the rise and fall of his brother with both precision and empathy. She had not shied away from the darker truths, yet her account also highlighted Kashyapa's vision and the complexity of his character.

When he finished, Moggallana set the scroll aside. "She has done justice to his story," he said quietly. "Let it be known to the court. The people deserve to remember him—for better or worse."

Ayodhya hesitated. "And what of the curse? The rumors persist.

Some believe the fortress should be destroyed entirely."

Moggallana shook his head. "No. Let it stand. Let it serve as a reminder of what ambition can achieve... and what it can destroy."

---

Decades later, Sigiriya had become a ghost of its former self. The jungle had claimed most of its structures, and the once-glimmering frescoes faded under the relentless passage of time. Yet, for those brave enough to venture close, the rock retained an aura of awe and unease.

Villagers spoke of strange lights flickering atop the summit and the sound of drums echoing through the night. They avoided the area, believing it to be sacred—or cursed. The "Lion Rock," as it came to be known, became a symbol of both human ingenuity and the perils of overreaching ambition.

In a small village near the rock, an elder recounted the tale of Kashyapa to a group of wide-eyed children gathered around a fire. His voice, tinged with both reverence and sorrow, wove the story into a cautionary tale.

"He was a king who sought to touch the heavens," the elder said, his gaze distant. "But in doing so, he angered the gods. His fortress was magnificent, but it could not protect him from his fate. Remember, children, greatness is a heavy burden. And the higher you rise, the farther you have to fall."

The flames crackled, casting shadows that danced across the faces of the listeners. Beyond them, the silhouette of Sigiriya loomed against the night sky, a silent sentinel guarding the secrets of the past.

# CHAPTER 41: VARUNI'S DISAPPEARANCE

The soft rustle of leaves under the dim light of a crescent moon whispered secrets across the abandoned grounds of Sigiriya. In the eerie stillness, once-bustling corridors lay barren, the echoes of hurried footsteps now replaced by the sigh of the wind. Somewhere within this desolation, Varuni was seen for the last time.

Moggallana's court buzzed with speculation. Soldiers murmured that Varuni had vanished under cover of night, her belongings untouched in her chamber, the lone candle extinguished as though by divine hands. Those who had trusted her as a mystic whispered that her departure signified her mission was complete—that she was a vessel of divine intervention, not bound to mortal ties.

Others were not so kind. The nobles, resentful of the power she had wielded, branded her a charlatan. They claimed her manipulations had driven Kashyapa into paranoia and madness. With her disappearance, the last vestiges of her influence dissolved, leaving behind only questions.

Moggallana himself offered no opinion, but his unease was

clear. Varuni had been a powerful presence—an enigma whose allegiance had never been fully known. Her vanishing left a void that even victory could not fill. Despite his triumph, he ordered her quarters searched thoroughly, but nothing of note was found. Only a single scroll rested on her desk, inscribed with cryptic symbols that no scribe could decipher.

In the villages below Sigiriya, tales of Varuni took on a life of their own. Some said she had been swallowed by the rock itself, her spirit now entwined with the cursed fortress. Others claimed she had fled to the mountains, carrying with her the knowledge of Kashyapa's downfall and secrets that could bring ruin to Moggallana's reign.

Ahalya, the chronicler who had documented Kashyapa's reign, found herself grappling with the mystery. Among the scrolls Varuni had left behind was a fragment that seemed to address her directly:

**"To those who write the future—truth is not what is written but what survives."**

Ahalya pondered the meaning of the words, her quill poised over parchment. Varuni's role in Kashyapa's rise and fall was undeniable, but how should it be recorded? As a prophet who foresaw the inevitable, or as a manipulator who shaped events to her will?

Despite her absence, Varuni's presence lingered. Those who had been close to Kashyapa spoke of her influence with both reverence and suspicion. Commander Vihara, recently released from imprisonment, reflected on her counsel during the most turbulent times. "She gave Kashyapa hope," he admitted, "but hope laced with fear is a dangerous gift."

Yet others believed she had always been working for Moggallana, sowing discord within the fortress to ensure its fall. A captured rebel confessed under duress that Varuni had met secretly with emissaries from Moggallana's camp months before the siege. The revelation, true or not, cast a long shadow over her legacy.

The last confirmed sighting of Varuni came from a servant who claimed to have seen her walking toward the Mirror Wall at twilight. She carried nothing but a small satchel and moved with a purpose that seemed otherworldly. "She looked as though she were following something," the servant said, trembling. "But there was nothing there."

The Mirror Wall, with its polished surface that once reflected the grandeur of Sigiriya, had become a place of dread. Workers claimed to see fleeting images of Kashyapa in its reflection, his eyes filled with despair. That Varuni had gone there—and vanished—only deepened the aura of mystery.

For Moggallana, Varuni's disappearance became both a relief and a warning. He declared Sigiriya unfit to serve as a capital, calling it a cursed monument to ambition. Yet, he could not shake the sense that Varuni's story was unfinished, that she remained a silent witness to his reign from some hidden vantage.

Years later, travelers spoke of a woman in the highlands who could summon visions and speak of kings with uncanny accuracy. They called her the Seer of the Peaks, though no one could confirm her identity. Those who sought her guidance often returned with riddles rather than answers.

Varuni's disappearance marked the end of an era. With Sigiriya abandoned and Kashyapa's legacy tarnished, her enigmatic role became a cautionary tale. To some, she was a mystic whose foresight was both a blessing and a curse. To others, she was a puppet master, her strings reaching further than anyone could imagine.

As Ahalya penned the final lines of her chronicle, she chose her words carefully:

*"In the annals of history, Varuni remains a shadow. Whether her intentions were pure or poisoned, her impact is undeniable. Perhaps it is fitting that she vanished into the same mystery from which she came, leaving us to question whether fate is guided by the divine, the human, or the unknown."*

And so, Varuni's name faded into legend, her disappearance an enduring mystery tied to the rise and fall of Sigiriya. In the halls of memory, she lingered—a ghostly figure whose presence would forever haunt the story of a king, a fortress, and a kingdom undone by ambition.

# CHAPTER 42: THE CURSE ENDURES

The monsoon rains arrived in Sigiriya like a mourning shroud, draping the land in a relentless gray. Torrents lashed against the fortress walls, carving jagged streams through the weathered rock. Water cascaded down the once-pristine frescoes, obscuring their vibrant hues and transforming them into blurred echoes of Kashyapa's dream. The skies rumbled ominously, as though lamenting the end of an era steeped in ambition and betrayal.

In the villages below, fear gripped the people. By day, they worked their fields in uneasy silence, casting wary glances toward the rock that loomed above them like a sentinel of doom. By night, their homes filled with whispered tales of curses and apparitions. Farmers swore they had seen flickering lights moving along the summit—ghostly flames that danced in defiance of the storm. Others spoke of mournful cries carried on the wind, a sound they claimed was the anguished spirit of Rajith.

To the villagers, Sigiriya was no longer the seat of a mighty king. It had become a haunted monument, a warning to those who dared defy the natural order.

It began with the workers who had fled during Kashyapa's

reign, those who had abandoned the fortress long before its fall. As they returned to their villages, they spoke of shadows that moved without a source and whispers that seemed to come from the stone itself. Some described a presence that had watched them while they worked—an oppressive weight that grew heavier with each passing day.

"Rajith walks the terraces at night," an elder told the gathered villagers one evening, his voice trembling. "He searches for justice. For retribution."

"What of King Kashyapa?" asked a young boy, his eyes wide with curiosity.

The elder's gaze darkened. "His spirit is bound to the throne he built. Until the rock crumbles, he will remain. Watching. Waiting."

Such stories spread like wildfire, igniting fear and awe in equal measure. Pilgrims avoided the rock entirely, and traders altered their routes to circumvent its shadow. Even those who doubted the supernatural dared not speak ill of the tales, for fear of inviting the curse upon themselves.

In Anuradhapura, King Moggallana's court buzzed with news of Sigiriya. Advisors urged him to repurpose the fortress, to make use of its strategic position and its grand design. But Moggallana, having seen the ruins with his own eyes, would hear none of it.

"That place is tainted," he declared to his council. "It reeks of blood and betrayal. Let it be reclaimed by the jungle. Let it stand as a monument to folly."

His decree was final. Sigiriya was abandoned, left to the mercy of time and nature. Vines crept up its stone walls, and trees took root in the once-meticulous gardens. The mirror wall, polished to perfection under Kashyapa's rule, began to crack and dull, reflecting not the grandeur of its creator but the inevitability of decay.

Yet even in abandonment, Sigiriya refused to be forgotten.

Travelers passing nearby claimed to hear footsteps in the empty corridors and faint laughter echoing from the summit. The stories grew darker with each retelling, transforming Kashyapa and Rajith into figures of legend.

As the years turned to decades, Sigiriya's tale spread far beyond the borders of Lanka. Scholars and poets alike took an interest in its history, weaving their own interpretations into its narrative. To some, it was a story of ambition unmatched by caution. To others, it was a tale of divine retribution, a reminder that no man could escape the consequences of his sins.

One such scholar, Ahalya, had returned to her village after Kashyapa's fall. With her she carried the records she had kept during his reign, though she rarely spoke of them. Only once, when pressed by a visiting monk, did she offer insight.

"Kashyapa was a man of vision," she said, her voice heavy with sorrow. "But his vision consumed him. He sought to rise above the heavens, yet he could not see the shadows beneath his own feet."

The monk nodded, his expression pensive. "And what of the curse? Does it endure?"

Ahalya hesitated before replying. "The curse is not in the rock. It is in the hearts of men. In their ambition. Their fear. Their inability to forgive."

Her words would later be recorded by the monk, ensuring that Kashyapa's story would be told not only as a cautionary tale but also as a reflection of the human condition.

Legends of the spirits dwelling in Sigiriya grew more elaborate with time. Hunters who dared venture too close reported seeing figures cloaked in mist, their eyes glowing with an otherworldly light. Some claimed the rock itself groaned underfoot, as though alive and resentful of their presence.

One night, a fisherman who had lost his way stumbled upon the base of the rock. He described hearing voices that seemed to speak directly to his soul.

"They called me by name," he said, trembling as he recounted his tale to the villagers. "They knew my fears. My regrets. They spoke of things I had done that no living man could know."

The villagers listened in silence, their fear palpable. None dared question the fisherman, for his terror was genuine. From that day forward, even the bravest among them avoided Sigiriya at all costs.

In the centuries that followed, Sigiriya became a symbol—not of triumph, but of tragedy. Its towering presence served as a reminder of Kashyapa's rise and fall, of his brilliance and his blindness. Travelers from distant lands came to see the ruins, drawn by the stories of ghosts and gods that had intertwined with its history.

Yet for all its decay, Sigiriya retained an air of majesty. The throne at its summit, though weathered and worn, still stood as a testament to Kashyapa's ambition. It was said that on moonless nights, the throne glowed faintly, as though lit from within by the remnants of the king's spirit.

Some believed Kashyapa watched over his creation still, bound by his love for the rock and his inability to let go of his failures. Others claimed the throne was cursed, that any who dared sit upon it would meet the same fate as its builder.

Whatever the truth, Sigiriya endured. Its walls, though crumbling, whispered stories to the wind. Its gardens, though overgrown, held echoes of their former beauty. And its people, though scattered, carried its legacy in their hearts.

For as long as Sigiriya stood, so too would the memory of Kashyapa. The king who dared defy the heavens. The king who dreamed too high. The king who fell.

# CHAPTER 43:
# LEGACY IN STONE

The sun dipped low over the plains, casting the ruins of Sigiriya in golden hues that shimmered like a fading crown. The once-magnificent fortress, built with Kashyapa's ambition and sealed with his blood, now stood as a silent monument to a forgotten era. Crumbling walls and weathered frescoes whispered secrets of its grandeur, while nature's vines crept over the stone, claiming it as their own.

In the centuries following Kashyapa's demise, Sigiriya became more than a ruin. It became a legend.

The villagers who lived in the shadow of the great rock told tales of the cursed king whose hubris angered the gods. They spoke of Kashyapa's ghost, wandering the heights of the fortress, his shadow visible under the light of a full moon. His throne—said to hold unspeakable power—remained hidden, guarded by his restless spirit and the lingering echoes of his paranoia.

Travelers from distant lands, drawn by the mystique of the rock, carried these stories back to their kingdoms. They described Sigiriya as a place where the lines between heaven and earth blurred, where man's ambition challenged the gods and was struck down. With each retelling, Kashyapa's story grew, shaped by the perspectives of those who told it. Some saw him as a tyrant, consumed by greed and cruelty; others viewed him as a tragic hero, undone by betrayal and his unrelenting pursuit of immortality.

In one version of the tale, Kashyapa's final moments were a defiant stand against the forces of fate, his death a noble sacrifice for his dream. In another, his end was a coward's fall, brought about by his own paranoia and the collapse of his empire. Chroniclers and poets debated endlessly, each seeking to immortalize the "Cursed King" in their own way.

Ahalya's record, unearthed centuries later, added layers to the narrative. In her account, she painted a picture of Kashyapa as a man of contradictions: a visionary architect and a flawed ruler, a protector and a destroyer. Her words held the weight of truth, but also the ambiguity of a survivor's perspective. She had chosen to hide the darkest secrets of his reign, leaving scholars to puzzle over the missing pieces.

One lingering mystery was the throne itself. Said to be crafted from black stone and embedded with jewels, it was never found. Treasure hunters searched the depths of Sigiriya's ruins, following maps and rumors, but the throne eluded them all. Some believed it had been hidden deliberately, its power too dangerous to reveal. Others whispered that it had been destroyed, consumed by the curse that lingered over the rock.

But the villagers believed it still existed, a relic of Kashyapa's undying will. On quiet nights, they claimed, you could hear the faint sound of his footsteps echoing through the corridors of the fortress, as if he were still guarding the seat of his power.

The ruins themselves stood as a testament to Kashyapa's ambition. The frescoes, though faded, retained a haunting beauty, their figures seeming to move in the flickering light of sunset. The water gardens, though choked with weeds, hinted at a mastery of engineering that had once brought life to an arid land. And the rock itself, towering and defiant, bore the scars of battles and time but refused to crumble.

Historians who visited Sigiriya marveled at its duality. It was both a symbol of human ingenuity and a cautionary tale of overreach. How had Kashyapa's vision, so grand and unparalleled, turned into a ghostly shadow of itself? Was it the weight of betrayal, the wrath of the gods, or the king's own flaws that had sealed its fate?

---

In time, Sigiriya became a place of pilgrimage for those seeking answers to questions that had no definitive answers. Poets came to draw inspiration from its eerie beauty. Philosophers meditated in its shadow, pondering the nature of ambition and legacy. Even rulers visited, hoping to glean some wisdom from Kashyapa's rise and fall.

Yet, for all its visitors, Sigiriya remained enigmatic. It seemed to exist out of time, a fragment of history that refused to fade entirely. The villagers who lived nearby often spoke of strange occurrences: lights flickering at the summit, voices carried by the wind, and the unshakable feeling of being watched.

---

One rainy evening, a scholar named Arun stood at the base of the rock, gazing up at its towering presence. He had spent years studying Kashyapa's life, piecing together fragments of history and myth. Now, standing in the shadow of the great fortress, he felt the weight of the king's story settle over him.

"What drove you, Kashyapa?" he murmured, his voice barely audible over the sound of the rain. "Was it fear? Pride? Or something more?"

The wind howled in response, carrying with it the faintest whisper of a voice. Arun shivered but remained still, his eyes fixed on the summit. He could almost see the king standing there, his figure framed by lightning, his gaze defiant even in death.

As the years turned into centuries, Sigiriya continued to stand, its legacy enduring in stories, songs, and the very stones that made up its walls. The "Lion Rock," as it came to be known, became a symbol of Sri Lanka's rich history, a place where the past and present intertwined.

Tourists from distant lands marveled at its majesty, unaware of the deeper currents of its history. Guides spoke of Kashyapa's brilliance and his tragic end, embellishing the tales to suit their audiences. And in the quiet corners of the ruins, where few dared to venture, the air seemed to hum with the presence of the king who had built it all.

Sigiriya, like Kashyapa, was a paradox. It was a place of beauty and sorrow, of triumph and ruin. It was a reminder of the heights to which humanity could soar and the depths to which it could fall.

And though Kashyapa's body had long since turned to dust, his spirit lingered—not as a ghost, but as an idea. A symbol of ambition's power and its cost. A story etched in stone, waiting for each new generation to uncover its truths and create new legends.

In the end, Sigiriya stood as it always had: defiant, enigmatic, and eternal. A legacy carved from rock, imbued with the dreams and failings of a king who dared to challenge the gods. A place where history and myth became one, and where the voice of Kashyapa could still be heard, whispering through the wind.

**"I am here. I will always be here."**

# AFTERWORD

The story of King Kashyapa and the fortress of Sigiriya is one steeped in mystery, legend, and the enduring allure of human ambition. Though much of what has been written in this novel is a product of imagination, it is inspired by the fragments of history that have survived through the centuries —archaeological wonders, ancient chronicles, and whispered folklore.

Sigiriya, with its towering presence and intricate artistry, is a testament to the ingenuity and determination of its creators. It reminds us of the lengths to which humanity will go to leave a mark on the world, to carve legacies into stone and defy the passage of time. But it also serves as a cautionary tale, hinting at the costs of ambition unrestrained by morality or foresight.

Kashyapa's story—whether viewed as that of a tyrant, a tragic figure, or a misunderstood visionary—captures the universal struggles of power, redemption, and legacy. He was a man of flesh and flaws, whose decisions shaped his reign and whose vision gave birth to a monument that continues to captivate.

In writing this novel, my hope was to give life to the voices that history often leaves unheard. What were the fears, hopes, and dreams of those who lived in Kashyapa's shadow? What drove them to support or betray him, and how did they make sense of the towering rock that loomed over their lives?

As Sigiriya continues to stand as a UNESCO World Heritage site and a symbol of Sri Lanka's rich history, it also invites us to ask questions about the stories we tell and the truths we seek. Who was Kashyapa? What was his dream for Sigiriya, and did he achieve it, even in death?

Thank you for journeying through the pages of this imagined history. May Kashyapa's tale remind us of the delicate balance between ambition and humility, legacy and hubris, and the eternal interplay of light and shadow in the human soul.

# ACKNOWLEDGEMENT

This book has been a labor of love, fueled by a passion for history, mythology, and storytelling. It would not have been possible without the support, guidance, and inspiration of so many people, to whom I owe a deep debt of gratitude.

To my wife, **Subhashini**, your unwavering belief in my vision and your boundless encouragement have been my greatest strength. Your insight and wisdom have enriched not only this story but every step of my journey. To our daughter, **Sasha**, your laughter and curiosity are constant reminders of life's most precious moments. This book is as much for you as it is for the legacy of storytelling itself.

A heartfelt thanks to my family and friends, who have been my first readers and my fiercest supporters. Your encouragement and honest feedback have helped shape this novel into what it is today.

To the countless historians, archaeologists, and researchers who have dedicated their lives to uncovering the mysteries of Sigiriya and King Kashyapa, your work has been a guiding light in my endeavor to breathe life into this historical figure. While this is a work of fiction, it is inspired by your dedication to preserving the truths of the past.

To my editor and publishing team, your tireless efforts and belief in this story have made it possible for Kashyapa's tale to reach the world. Your keen eyes and thoughtful input have brought clarity and polish to these pages.

Finally, to you, the reader—thank you for taking this journey with me. It is your imagination and curiosity that give meaning to these words. May you find in Kashyapa's story a reflection of humanity's timeless struggles and aspirations, and may Sigiriya's majesty continue to inspire.

With gratitude,
**D. Deckker**

# ABOUT THE AUTHOR

## D. Deckker

Dinesh Deckker is a seasoned expert in digital marketing, boasting more than 20 years of experience in the industry. His strong academic foundation includes a BA in Business Management from Wrexham University (UK), a Bachelor of Computer Science from IIC University (Cambodia), an MBA from the University of Gloucestershire (UK), and ongoing PhD studies in Marketing.

Deckker's career is as versatile as his academic pursuits. He is also a prolific author, having written over 100+ books across various subjects.

He has further honed his writing skills through a variety of specialized courses. His qualifications include:

Children Acquiring Literacy Naturally from UC Santa Cruz, USA

Creative Writing Specialization from Wesleyan University, USA

Writing for Young Readers Commonwealth Education Trust

Introduction to Early Childhood from The State University of

New York

Introduction to Psychology from Yale University

Academic English: Writing Specialization University of California, Irvine,

Writing and Editing Specialization from University of Michigan

Writing and Editing: Word Choice University of Michigan

Sharpened Visions: A Poetry Workshop from CalArts, USA

Grammar and Punctuation from University of California, Irvine, USA

Teaching Writing Specialization from Johns Hopkins University

Advanced Writing from University of California, Irvine, USA

English for Journalism from University of Pennsylvania, USA

Creative Writing: The Craft of Character from Wesleyan University, USA

Creative Writing: The Craft of Setting from Wesleyan University

Creative Writing: The Craft of Plot from Wesleyan University, USA

Creative Writing: The Craft of Style from Wesleyan University, USA

Dinesh's diverse educational background and commitment to lifelong learning have equipped him with a deep understanding of various writing styles and educational techniques. His works often reflect his passion for storytelling, education, and technology, making him a versatile and engaging author.

# BOOKS BY THIS AUTHOR

## The Complete Guide To Greek Mythology: Gods, Heroes, And The Mysteries Of Olympus

Unveil the fascinating world of Greek mythology with The Complete Guide to Greek Mythology: Gods, Heroes, and the Mysteries of Olympus. This comprehensive guide explores the timeless myths that have shaped Western culture for millennia.

## Devadatta - The Rebel Monk: A Novel Of Redemption

What drives a man to rebel against one of history's greatest teachers? Devadatta - The Rebel Monk by D. Deckker reimagines the life of Siddhartha's infamous cousin and disciple, exploring the ambition and inner conflict that led to his betrayal.

Follow Devadatta on a journey from devoted monk to divisive rebel, grappling with jealousy, power, and his quest for enlightenment. Rich in historical detail and emotional depth, this novel uncovers the humanity of a man often dismissed as a villain.

## The Light Of Bethlehem: A Story Of Hope And Light - Nativity Story Novel

Step into the timeless story of Bethlehem with this deeply human retelling of the Nativity. The Light of Bethlehem invites readers to witness the miracle through the eyes of those who were there—Mary, Joseph, the shepherds, and the wise men. This novel beautifully captures their courage, love, and sacrifice, weaving a rich tapestry of hope and resilience.

## Silent Night: A Christmas Horror

Mia and her friends were hoping for a fun-filled Christmas getaway at a remote lodge, surrounded by snow and holiday cheer. But as a powerful blizzard closes in, the lodge becomes a place of mystery and fear. Strange symbols, eerie noises, and an unsettling legend start to unravel the group's sense of safety.

Made in the USA
Columbia, SC
22 January 2025

52235557R00111